BULLETS ON BUNCHGRASS

BULLETS ON BUNCHGRASS

Louis Trimble

Chivers
Bath, England

•

Thorndike Press
Waterville, Maine USA

11/03 GG 2395

This Large Print edition is published by BBC Audiobooks Ltd, England, and by Thorndike Press, USA.

Published in 2003 in the U.K. by arrangement with the author c/o Golden West Literary Agency.

Published in 2003 in the U.S. by arrangement with Golden West Literary Agency.

U.K. Hardcover   ISBN 0–7540–7269–X (Chivers Large Print)
U.K. Softcover   ISBN 0–7540–7270–3 (Camden Large Print)
U.S. Softcover   ISBN 0–7862–5413–0 (Nightingale Series)

The text of this Large Print edition is unabridged.
Other aspects of the book may vary from the original edition.

Set in 16 pt. New Times Roman.

Printed in Great Britain on acid-free paper.

British Library Cataloguing in Publication Data available

Library of Congress Cataloging-in-Publication Data

Trimble, Louis, 1917–
    Bullets on Bunchgrass / Louis Trimble.
        p. cm.
    ISBN 0–7862–5413–0 (lg. print : sc : alk. paper)
    1. Ranch life—Fiction. 2. Cattle stealing—Fiction.
    3. Large type books. I. Title.
PS3570.R519B85 2003
813'.54—dc21   2003047357

CHAPTER ONE

Carr had barely managed to finish shaving the five-day growth of beard from his still badly bruised face when he heard Peak coming in the spring wagon. Drawn by the urgency in the way the old man was yelling at the team to hurry, he walked outside into the strong May sunshine. In a moment Peak appeared at the end of the quarter-mile trail that led from Carr's L-in-C to the main road, the loaded wagon swaying, the bay team in a lather.

Seeing Carr, Peak jerked the team to a halt near the rear porch where he stood. 'Amighty, Carr! Hell's going to pop in town if that fool sheriff don't do something.'

He climbed from the wagon stiffly and yelled for Ned Watts as Carr watched, then he started for the house. If Peak was excited enough to overlook the fact that he was out of bed without Doc Mason's approval, Carr thought, then something was definitely wrong.

'What's going on?' Carr asked the old man.

'Well, I got a message for you from the sheriff's sister,' Peak blurted out, panting between words as if he had run as fast as the horses. 'Elsa said to tell you that Mort Ogle and Purvis and Jerry Dyke—and a half a dozen others—are listening to that scrawny Tindle and have been, off and on, since yesterday—

1

and right about now, they're spoiling for trouble. I found 'em in the Buckhorn Saloon myself just a while ago and that little whelp was haranguing 'em about Pat Tyler and—'

'What about Elsa?' Carr interrupted.

'She said if you could come to town and talk to her brother about Pat, maybe you could stop those fools.'

Carr doubted that those were Elsa's exact words. He said, 'That's why I got up, to go see Nash. But what does Tindle want to do with Pat?'

Peak spat and looked toward the barn. Ned Watts was just coming around it, moving as fast as his short legs and round body would allow.

'Put the team away, will you, Ned?' he yelled, without answering Carr's question. 'And saddle up. We're going to town.'

'There's no need,' Carr said. 'It only takes one to talk to the sheriff.'

'That's what you think. If Tindle tries to start something—what then?' Peak glared at him. 'He's in the saloon now yelling that the law's too slow and there ain't no reason to wait for court. Since Pat Tyler confessed to rustling beef, he ought to be strung up. That's what Tindle wants to do.'

'What's the sheriff doing?' Carr broke in.

'According to Elsa, he told Tindle to shut up and figured since it was the law talking everything was taken care of. Besides, Tindle

2

ain't breaking no law just talking.'

'That's the way Nash would look at it,' Carr murmured. He went into the house, moving slowly because he was still unsure of himself after spending nearly all of the last five days on his back in bed.

Peak followed him. 'You sure you can make this? Doc Mason said it'd be a week or better.'

'I'm sure,' Carr said. 'What's there to keep me in bed?'

Peak trailed him to the bedroom where he got into his vest and strapped his gunbelt around his waist. 'Nothing but two cracked ribs from that fall off your horse.' The old man's voice was sour with sarcasm. 'Nothing but a beating from that Griff fellow that had you out of your head two days in the hospital. I don't know, Carr. Maybe you ought to—'

Carr turned on him almost savagely. 'Pat Tyler's in jail, Peak. I took that beating from Griff and I took that fall from my horse trying to help him. Do you think I'll stand by now and see him lynched because the sheriff is too big a fool to believe anyone would break his law?'

'All right,' Peak said. 'Let's ride.'

Even though Carr's buckskin was an easy riding horse, he found every step a jolt to his still-sore body. Peak kept glancing anxiously at him, noting that his face had grown even leaner than usual so that the cheekbones pulled the skin taut over the sharp bone structure of his face.

'What you going to tell Nash?' he demanded as they started onto the wagon road.

Carr studied the timber that lined the road thickly on either side. He had spent the last three days conscious enough to think about this and now he said slowly, 'I'm going to try to make Nash see that Neil Griff and that land agent friend of his, Finley, have something to do with Pat's rustling.'

Old Peak swore sharply. 'Pat ain't the kind to rustle nobody's beef. Especially that belonging to his friends.'

'I know,' Carr agreed quietly. He was silent a moment, trying to adjust himself to the horse's gait. 'And he didn't start until about the time this Griff showed up here last week. And if Griff has nothing to do with it, why did he and Finley try to work me into a fight in a game of cards right after I discovered Pat was rustling? Or why, when I helped Pat so he wouldn't get caught at it the next day, did Griff beat me so bad when I caught him spying from the west ridge?'

He winced, remembering the fight. 'He gave me a boxing lesson. He could have beat me in a fair fight, I think. But he had to make sure and hold a gun on me while he knocked the sap out of me before he'd fight even.'

He looked at both Ned and Peak. 'Why? What's Griff's stake in this?'

Old Peak snorted. 'You think Nash will listen to you, Carr? What's he done about Griff showing up with a title to Pat's T!Over and asking for a dispossess warrant?'

Carr turned toward him sharply. 'Griff did what?'

'Heard it yesterday,' Peak said. 'But I wasn't going to tell you when you were in bed like that. Pat no sooner goes and turns himself in to Nash than Griff shows up with title to Pat's place.'

'My God,' Carr half whispered. 'Can't Nash see anything?'

'Pat's story don't mean nothing to Nash— Pat's a confessed rustler, ain't he? His word don't carry weight now.'

Carr was silent, turning this latest news over in his mind, trying to fit it into the pattern that he had formed off Griff's actions while lying in bed. The man was clever, he thought. Clever enough to make whatever he was doing appear to be within the law—and thus not where Nash would pay attention to it.

There was nothing he could put a finger on and say to Nash, 'Griff did it this way.' It was all feeling, all guesswork, he realized. But Griff's crookedness was as strong a certainty inside him as was the knowledge that Pat Tyler was in jail on a rustling warrant with men he had considered his friends planning to lynch him.

Now they were dropping down the easy

grade and turning toward Buckhorn where it sprawled out from the hills. When they arrived, the single dusty main street was almost empty. The only sign of life except for a spring wagon before the Mercantile was a bunched group of horses tied in front of the Buckhorn Saloon.

'You stay in there,' Carr told the men, indicating the saloon. 'Maybe Tindle won't have so much to say with someone else around.' He looked at the mild, round-faced Ned Watts. 'And keep Peak from starting anything.'

'Yep.' Ned Watts said. It was a full speech for him.

Carr rode on, pulled up in front of the log jail building long enough to read the 'Back at Four' sign on the closed door, swung his horse about and rode to the cross street and turned north. A half block and he went west again, up the alley that separated the four-cell jail from the small house where Sim Nash lived with his sister. Leaving his horse in the yard, Carr walked as unhurriedly as he could to the kitchen door.

Elsa Nash opened the door to his knock. There was gladness in her dark eyes at seeing him but a twist of fright was there also.

'Carr, are you all right?'

'I got your message,' he said in a low voice. 'I came to see your brother.' He could make out the long, thin back of Sim Nash seated at the kitchen table. Carr took her hands in his. 'Things could be worse,' he said softly.

'Yes,' she said bitterly. 'Tindle's bullet could have hit you the other day instead of making your horse throw you.'

'Shooting a man is against the law,' Carr said loudly, for Nash to hear. 'Tindle would never do that.' He walked into the kitchen as Elsa stepped aside.

Nash came to his feet and turned, his thin face flushed, the muscles around his long jaw drawn taut. 'Meaning what, Lindon?'

Carr took off his hat and stood a moment, fighting back his anger. Somehow he and Nash had never seen eye to eye in the little over a year since Nash had come to Buckhorn. And since the trouble, Carr had felt a definite antagonism whenever they met.

He said now, quietly, 'Meaning I hear that Tindle is stirring the men up in town, Sheriff, to lynch Pat. I came to ask your help.'

Nash looked contemptuously at Carr and resumed his seat at the table. Elsa motioned Carr to a seat and went to get him a cup of coffee. He watched her go, noting the fine, graceful movements of her tall body. Then he turned his attention once more to the sheriff.

'I gave those men a warning this morning,' Nash said. 'I'm the law here, Lindon, and I can handle any trouble that comes up.'

Carr forced himself to be calm. Riling Nash would get him nowhere. 'I came to ask your

7

help,' he repeated. 'Surely the fact that Griff has shown up with a title to Pat's land has some meaning.'

Nash was not a truculent man, and he spoke now without any belligerence in his voice. But there was a coldness in his tone that carried more force than shouting would have. 'You've come to me before about Griff, Lindon. And I've said before that I must abide by the law. The title he has is legal. It isn't up to me to question how he got it.'

Carr leaned over the table, ignoring his coffee. 'Sheriff, the law has no meaning unless it is tempered with justice. And where is the justice in Pat Tyler being in jail, his land held by someone else? Give him a chance to prove that he was put into the position of rustling under duress—as he claims. Give him into my custody long enough to—'

'Lindon, even if it were legal, I would hardly hand a confessed criminal into the hands of one who could be charged as an accomplice.' His voice dropped the words with finality. 'I don't tell you how to run your cattle; don't try to tell me how to run the law.'

Elsa Nash turned from the stove and stood before her brother. 'Sim, as the law you are required to listen to Carr as you would to anyone else.'

Nash got to his feet, his face white. Then he drew a deep breath, picked up his hat, and started for the door. 'Come to my office, then, if you have something to say, Lindon.'

Carr sat watching him go. Then he reached out to lift his coffee cup. Elsa put out her hand and caught his arm. He was trembling.

'No man ever learned anything being preached at,' she said to him softly. 'Talking to Sim is wasting your strength.'

Carr turned to her. She resembled her brother but her expression was soft where his was hard, her mouth warm and full where his was cold. He reached out and touched her dark hair where a strand fell across her cheek.

'I gather you heard about my falling from the horse. I'm glad you did. I didn't want you to think I hadn't come to see you because of—him.'

'Peak told me,' she said. 'But I would have come up there if you hadn't appeared soon.' She smiled gently. 'Carr, don't you know me well enough by now? Do you think my love is so fragile that even Sim could destroy it?'

She loved her brother, he knew, and he could not blame her for this, no matter what he might think of Sim Nash personally. The man had proved his worth when he had been brought in over a year before to clean the town of riffraff left as the backwash of a short-lived gold strike in the mountains. Carr could not blame her, but the situation bothered him a great deal.

'What will happen if I have to go against your brother, Elsa?'

9

She rose and he followed her, waiting for her answer. Stopping by the door, she lifted her face to his. 'Don't, Carr. Try to understand Sim. He has handled things like this before.'

'Yet you sent a message to me—warning me.'

'Because Sim is so much the law that sometimes he is blinded by it,' she said. 'And because Pat Tyler is your friend and Sim is just one man. Can't you see, Carr? If you could work with him—or he with you—it would be so much better.'

'Better,' he agreed. 'I asked today. I'm going over to ask again. But if I should fail—if I should have to go against him?'

'Carr,' she said softly, 'I don't know. I don't know.' She reached her hands up to draw his face down to hers. 'But I'd try to understand, Carr.'

Her lips were on his and her body, warm, alive, pressed against him with a hunger that was a little frightening. He knew that in this woman he had met and come to love in so short a time there was a strong, violent nature. But he had never known her to be quite like this before.

It was she who broke away at last. 'I'd try to understand,' she repeated. Her eyes dropped from his and she flushed a little. Then she lifted her head and looked squarely at him. 'I can only say that what I can do to help, I will do. Remember that I've lived with Sim Nash all my life. There are things that I know how to do—when I must.'

'I'll remember,' he said. 'I may have to.' And taking his hat, he walked away.

CHAPTER TWO

Carr entered Nash's office and took a chair to one side of the desk. He forced himself to keep his temper down. This was his chance to say what there was to say and he wouldn't make it better by angering Nash more than he already had.

Carefully, he shaped a cigarette and lighted it. Then he said, 'Sheriff, Pat Tyler came to town voluntarily and gave himself up. You asked no questions about why he should do that—all you could think of was that he confessed to rustling beef from the valley.'

Nash's eyes were cold on him. 'It's obvious enough, isn't it? Tyler was seen rustling. He shot at Ogle and Purvis—at you, for that matter. Cattle have been found in the Bowl at the head of Rustler's Trail.'

Carr bit back a short answer. When he spoke he sounded almost weary. 'And so was a campfire with a few things that men have identified as coming from Pat Tyler's house. Lots of "evidence" has turned up since he was put in jail. Men who hardly knew him are suddenly willing to swear all sorts of things. Surely, you've had enough law experience to know how little such things mean.'

Nash flushed. He was silent a moment and when he spoke his voice was calm. 'Just what did you come to tell me, Lindon?'

Carr leaned forward and threw his half-smoked cigarette into the spittoon. 'This. A week ago I was hunting strays up the slope by Rustler's Trail. I saw a small herd being pushed up there and tried to catch the man who was driving them. He got into the timber on the west side and took a shot at me. I lost him for a while, but I trailed him to town because he was riding a horse with a splayed foot. Pat Tyler was in town. He has a horse with a splayed foot, and I tried to talk to him about it.'

Carr added flatly, 'I didn't jump to the conclusion that he had turned from a good neighbor and friend into a rustler. I figured if Pat had done something like that, there was a reason. I tried to find out what it was.'

Nash fixed a cigarette and smoked quietly. 'Go on,' he said in an expressionless voice.

Carr continued, 'I went to the Buckhorn Saloon to wait him out and ride home with him that night. He was in a card game with Finley and a stranger—who turned out to be this Neil Griff. I sat in with them on Finley's invitation. You know what kind of a deal that was.'

12

Nash's voice was dry as he answered. 'You accused Griff of throwing hands so you could win the pots from him. When he refused to take the money you claimed was his, and not yours, you picked a fight with him. Then, when I stopped it, you made a complaint to me. It didn't make sense and it still doesn't.'

'Not much,' Carr agreed. As Nash had said it, it made no sense at all. 'I still claim he was trying to get me into a fight. Before I saw you here afterward, he came outside and prodded me some more.'

'What for?' Nash asked. 'Why should a stranger pick a fight with you?'

'Why did all this start just about the time he came to town?' Carr countered. 'Sheriff, I say that somehow Griff is behind all this. He's behind whatever Pat was doing.'

'Tyler is over twenty-one,' Nash answered. 'Can another man make a person rustle his friends' cattle and shoot at them?'

Carr said tiredly, 'I know that Pat wouldn't say anything that night except to hint that I should watch out for Griff. And the next day I watched and saw the same thing happening. Only this time Pat was nearly caught when Ogle, with Dyke and Purvis, came riding into the valley to check their beef.'

'Ah,' Nash said softly, 'then you admit it was Tyler.'

Carr brushed it aside with a gesture of his hand. 'I do because I saw him this time.' He met the sheriff's gaze squarely. 'You already know that. I helped him break up the herd and scatter them to make it look like he was hunting strays. Pat is my friend and I wanted to find out why he was doing it. If I had let Ogle and the others catch him, I wasn't sure what might happen.'

'And that makes you an accomplice in the eyes of the law,' Nash murmured. 'Go on, Lindon.'

Carr took the time to roll another cigarette before continuing. Finally he said, 'After that, I rode up the west ridge. In trailing Pat that day, I found the tracks of two men who had been watching him. That didn't make much sense—unless they were watching to make sure he *did* rustle the beef.'

'Why?' Nash asked easily.

'I'm here to find out why,' Carr said shortly. 'I think I'm right, because when I crawled up the west ridge,· there was another watcher there—with a carbine.'

'It's the logical place to watch the valley from,' Nash agreed.

'You've heard the rest of this,' Carr said. 'It was Griff—and he was aching for a fight. He held me with a gun and beat me.'

'And you spent three days in the hospital,' Nash murmured. 'I know. So he fought you because you accused him of cheating himself in the Buckhorn. He claims he was out looking over the land he's been having Ed Finley buy

14

for him when you rode up and called him.'

'I know what he claims,' Carr said. 'The point is that he was looking over the valley, not his own holdings. All right, when I got out of the hospital, I rode home to find Tindle taking Ogle and Dyke and Purvis into the valley. He claimed he had been riding there and saw someone rounding up their beef—along with Pat's and mine—and pushing it up Rustler's Trail. I joined them and we went after the man. We never did get close enough to see who it was and—'

Nash interrupted. 'According to Ogle, you saw a blond man wearing a fancy vest like the one Tyler wears most of the time. When you were close enough to hail him, he shot at you and broke for it.'

'And we shot at him,' Carr said simply. 'Or one of us did. I think it was Tindle, but I won't swear to that. We found the man's hat and the tracks of a splayfooted horse.'

'Evidence enough for Ogle to ride to me as he did,' Nash said.

Carr said bitterly, 'And because I tried to cool them down, they put Tindle out to guard me.' He studied the sheriff and found no interest there, just a calm waiting.

'All right, I did ride to see Pat. I was going to make him explain or bring him in to you. Only,' he added disgustedly, 'I handled Tindle wrong and he took a shot at me. My horse bolted and I went down. After the beating I

15

took from Griff, the fall was too much. It finished cracking two of my ribs and I was in bed again.'

Nash nodded. 'They had no right to guard a man. But under the circumstances, it seemed a wise thing to do. How were they to know you wouldn't try to help Tyler get out of the country?'

'They know me better than that.'

'They thought they knew Tyler well, too, Lindon. But that same day he came to town and confessed to having rustled the cattle. So Ogle's interpretation of the evidence was right.'

Carr said wearily, 'Did it ever occur to any of you to ask Pat why he did it? Did anyone give him a chance to explain?'

'He gave me a story,' Nash said. His voice was dry, almost scornful. 'And he claims he was being held a prisoner by Griff in the mountains when you and Ogle and the others were shooting at him on the trail. He says it wasn't him.'

'Ah,' Carr said and there was vast relief in his voice. Then he saw the expressionless face before him and the relief turned to bitterness. 'And you refuse to believe him?'

'It isn't up to me,' Nash said. 'There's been a warrant sworn. He's in jail on that warrant. He can defend himself at his trial.'

'If there *is* a trial,' Carr said. 'You know what's going on in town. Why do you think

16

they're meeting?'

'I told you before that I'm the law,' Nash said. 'I can handle my own affairs.'

To Carr his words meant that his mind was made up and nothing Carr could say would change it. He could understand the workings of Nash's mind to this extent: In Ogle he had a reliable witness; in Pat Tyler he had a self-confessed rustler. And the fact that Carr was a friend of Tyler's and, admittedly, had helped him hide his rustling once would not make Nash look on him as an unprejudiced witness. But seeing Nash's point of view didn't make it any more acceptable.

Carr rose. 'What Pat said about Griff holding him prisoner, what I said about finding Griff watching and finding the tracks of two other people—those things have no meaning? And with Griff having title to Pat's land. Surely—'

'I haven't forgotten them,' Nash said.

'Sheriff, I ask again that you give Pat Tyler a chance to help himself, not leave him to be strung up like a common horse thief.'

'There'll be no stringing,' Nash said shortly. He looked bleakly at Carr. 'Remember, Lindon, I could jail you as an accomplice—on your own admission. You've had your say. Now I have work to do.'

It was a curt dismissal. Carr started for the door, turned, then swung about and strode away. The anger in him was too violent to risk

17

speech. From Nash's attitude, he knew that the sheriff would not accept anything he might say or do, unless he had absolute proof. Carr had a strong respect for the law. He had always had a strong respect for Sim Nash, despite his dislike for the man himself. But now, after this . . .

The sun was slanting strongly when Carr pushed through the doors into the Buckhorn Saloon. It was a dim, cool place and, at this hour, shortly before supper, well filled with townsmen and ranchers. Carr walked past the long bar, his eyes searching the dark recesses at the rear. Gilly Dall, the owner, saw him and stopped wiping at the glass he held in his hand. His eyes traveled from Carr to the far corner.

'Evening, Gilly,' Carr said. 'My boys here?'

'Straight back,' Gilly Dall said, going back to his wiping.

Carr found old Peak and Ned Watts nursing glasses of beer and pretending to play a game of cribbage. Peak took a long look at Carr as he came up.

'You been riling yourself,' the old man said. 'Talk did no good?'

'No good,' Carr said briefly. 'What about the meeting?'

Ned Watts jerked his head toward the corner at which Gilly Dall had glanced upon first seeing Carr. Peak said, 'Been at it all afternoon. Tindle ain't talking loud, but he's steady. Some of 'em are getting drunk, too.'

18

'Wait here,' Carr said, and turned away. He walked through a cluster of small card tables to where Tindle was striding up and down in front of a group of about a dozen men. Carr saw Mort Ogle, his heavy face showing red from his having drunk too much whiskey. Flanking him were Larry Purvis, his lantern jaw set tight, and Jerry Dyke looking like a minister on a holiday. Both of them looked a little the worse for wear, and Carr wondered if they had to keep drinking to stomach Tindle.

Tindle was a little man with a bull's voice, though now he had it pitched low. One of the fringe ranchers who lived off roundups and occasional cuttings of dogies from other men's herds, Tindle had been one of the first to sell his scrub timberland to Ed Finley, the land agent. But as far as Carr could tell, he still lived on the place, though he spent most of his time in town.

Carr was within five feet of him before he could hear Tindle's words.

'I seen courts before,' he was saying, 'and them that has money can get off scot free. Tyler's still got powerful friends, I tell you, and with the sheriff's sister going with Lindon, it won't surprise me if—'

Putting out a hand, Carr took Tindle by the shoulder and slowly twisted him around.

'Repeat that,' he said.

Tindle's narrow face whitened and he twisted sharply, freeing himself and darting

19

sideways, out of Carr's reach. Carr looked disgustedly at him and then at Mort Ogle. 'Private meeting?' he asked the latter.

Ogle's hoarse voice was deep, almost inaudible. 'Yes.'

Carr said in the same quiet tone, 'I don't like people who've called me friend to put scum like Tindle out to guard me. I ride where I please when I please.'

The liquor in Ogle made his face even redder than usual. He said belligerently, 'You'd done the same in my place.'

'No,' Carr argued softly. 'If I have a friend, I trust him.'

'Even when he's a rustler,' Tindle said quickly.

Carr didn't bother to look at him. 'Even when he's a rustler,' Carr said levelly. 'I'd be curious to know why a friend suddenly turned that way. I'd want to know his side of it.'

Tindle made a laughing sound. 'His side—Tyler's side!'

'What side has Tyler got?' Larry Purvis demanded, looking at Ogle for approval.

'No side,' Ogle said in his rumbling voice.

'No side,' Tindle echoed. 'Like I said, we seen him clear as day, pushing beef up Rustler's Trail.' He pushed his face in Carr's direction. 'You was there. He took a shot at us, didn't he?'

Carr moved quickly and Tindle's voice gurgled off as he was hoisted clear of the floor.

Carr pushed him away contemptuously. 'I saw a man riding too far ahead to be sure who it was.' He stopped, feeling the hopelessness he had felt with the sheriff. These men were a blank wall to his words. He saw nothing but stubborn righteousness on Mort Ogle's face. What was done was done, as far as Ogle was concerned, and Carr knew that the why of it didn't interest him. 'I didn't see Pat Tyler,' Carr finished.

'We found his hat,' Ogle reminded him. 'We found the marks of that splayfooted horse he rides.'

'He'll twist evidence in court,' Tindle said shrilly. 'Like I told you.'

Carr's careful control broke under the nagging insistence of the man's voice. He took a step toward Tindle, then moved sideways. Tindle ducked too soon and outfoxed himself, running into Carr as he changed direction. He made a screeching sound as Carr slapped him with his open hand, knocking him to the floor, where he rolled frantically toward Ogle.

Carr looked at Ogle and the pity in his eyes was obvious. 'Go ahead and make fools of yourselves by listening to him. But when Griff and his crew have you over a barrel, remember that you spent your time listening to Tindle.'

'What's Griff got to do with this?' Purvis demanded.

'He's sitting on the T-Over,' Carr said. 'He was watching Pat push our beef up the Trail

21

the day I found him and he beat me. Now he's got the Saddle.' He saw no comprehension of what that might mean in the eyes of Ogle or the other ranchers who shared the valley graze. 'Pat was your friend—and you sit by and let someone take his land from him. You—' He stopped, realizing the foolishness of this. His voice was low and harsh as he added, 'While you sit and plan to take his life away.' His eyes were on Ogle's face. 'You can't wait for Pat to come to trial, can you, Mort?'

'The law is too slow,' Ogle said, his voice dogged with liquor. 'What I saw is trial enough.'

Carr felt a great pity for this man. He doubted if Ogle could shoot anyone unless driven to it in self-defense. Yet here he was, drinking heavily and listening to Tindle, in an effort to rouse himself to hang someone—and too frightened to see that it was just as much murder as shooting would be.

Ogle stood up, swaying slightly. 'What call you got to defend Pat?' he demanded. His voice had thickened as if the movement had worked the whiskey around in him. 'He took your beef, didn't he? He shot at you, didn't he?'

Carr could feel a stirring run through the group. They were beginning to get ugly now, and he realized that his coming had only made them worse. Without answering, he turned away, lifted a hand to Peak and Ned Watts, and walked from the saloon.

He was halfway across the street when he saw three men riding down from the sheriff's office. He recognized Ed Finley, because of his great bulk in the saddle. Neil Griff rode on one side of him, a big man, solid, looking part of the fine black beneath him. Next to Griff was Sim Nash, looking neither to the right nor left.

Carr watched them approach and then deliberately stepped up by Nash's horse. 'Sheriff,' he said urgently, 'you can't leave town now.'

Nash looked down at him with no expression. 'Running my business again, Lindon?'

Carr glanced past him and saw the amused smile on Griff's craggy face. 'I'm afraid your business will have to wait, Lindon. The sheriff has some of mine to take care of.'

'They're getting riled in there,' Carr said, jerking a hand toward the saloon. 'If you want a lynching on your hands . . .'

'I told you that was taken care of,' Nash said coldly. 'Stand aside, Lindon.'

Carr reached up and caught the horse's bridle. 'Where are you going?'

'Your affair? It happens that your friend Tyler's men won't honor Griff's dispossess. I'm going to serve it. Now stand aside.'

Carr fell back, the helplessness flooding in on him again. Griff tipped his hat in mock

23

sympathy as he rode on, flanked by Nash and the fat Finley, who had been silent for once in his life. Carr watched them go, until dimness hid them at the lower edge of town. Then he hurried to the sidewalk where Peak and Ned Watts waited. Peak was dropping his hand reluctantly from his gun.

'The fool!' Carr said. 'That's the oldest trick in the world. Can't Nash see that he's being taken out of town on purpose tonight?'

'The law says he serves dispossesses, I reckon,' Peak said dryly. 'It don't say he protects rustlers, maybe.' He spat into the dirt of the street. 'Pat's got three men up there and Griff has a dozen that's been driving cattle from the railhead across the Bunchgrass ever since he showed up here.'

Carr nodded. Griff could have forced his way in had he wanted to. But the shrewd move, as Carr saw it, was to appeal to the law for help. He thought of the three T-Over men up in the hills and he knew that they would fight one or a dozen—Griff or the sheriff or anyone else who tried to take away the ranch that had been their home as long as he could remember. He swore.

'Peak, you and Ned ride. Take the shortcut and—' Carr saw people moving about him, hurrying or drifting along the sidewalk as it suited them, and he took both men by the arm and pulled them to the corner of the hotel. 'If you take the switchback,' he said, 'you can beat

24

Griff and his crew to T-Over. Tell Marcus and Bettle and Milo Carter to get their stuff and move over to my place. They'll start a fracas if you don't talk fast to them.'

'Might be a good thing to see,' Peak suggested.

'Might help,' Ned Watts said.

'Later,' Carr replied almost roughly. 'Right now I want you to get them there and then come back here.' He bent by the corner of the building and drew a rough map of the town. 'Bring them with you and put them here— under those trees just where the last cross street comes. Then you and Ned ride up this alley to the sheriff's barn. There'll be an extra horse there, saddled. When you get there, give me the coyote signal. I'll be waiting.'

'Waiting for what?'

'Not for the law,' Carr said angrily, but softly. 'When I hear your signal, I'll free Pat and we'll ride.'

Old Peak's eyes gleamed. 'Glory be!' he said. 'And what then?'

'And then,' Carr said, 'we'll head for the high country, up to the old outlaw hangout.' He added bleakly, 'We'll be wanted by the law too.'

CHAPTER THREE

Neil Griff rode easily alongside Sheriff Nash as they climbed the gentle slope of the wagon road. 'Thanks for doing this, Sheriff,' he said. 'I've been in places where a stranger would have had a hard time getting his case heard.'

'The law is impartial,' Nash said briefly. He rode stiffly as if his thin body might break should he let it relax for a moment. He added in his expressionless voice, 'But a lot of people besides Lindon won't like my doing this.'

'Duty,' murmured Griff. He smiled and glanced at Nash. 'They won't like it because I'm a stranger—or because of my fight with Lindon?'

'Both—and more,' Nash replied bluntly. 'Tyler claims you forced him into rustling and that the day he was supposed to have shot at Ogle and his men he was being held a prisoner by one of your men in the high country.' It was obvious that Nash was probing for information. 'When that kind of talk goes around, Griff, there'll be complaints.'

Griff's smile turned into an easy laugh. 'I'd call it a case of sour grapes, Sheriff. I made a deal with Tyler in Spokane Falls for his ranch. You saw my title; it's perfectly legal. My guess is that when he got back home he realized he had acted too quickly and thought he'd wriggle out of the bargain by rustling and pinning it on me. That's my theory.'

'I have a different one, Sheriff.' Ed Finley said. 'It seems to me that Tyler was trying to make a clean-up and get out of the country now that he no longer owns T-Over. But he wasn't clever enough to be a criminal and got nervous and gave himself up.' His own oratory always had a hypnotizing effect on Finley and now, as uncomfortable as he was whenever he had to compress his bulk into a saddle, he let his voice soar on. 'It doesn't make Tyler less guilty. In fact it might make him more dangerous. A cornered man is a frightened man and—'

'You talk too much,' Neil Griff said briefly. He turned to the sheriff as Finley's voice trailed away. 'Whatever the reason, Sheriff, Tyler's guilt is incontestable.'

'That's for the court to decide,' Nash said.

Griff nodded. They were at the top of the trail now, traveling through the alley of heavy spruce and fir that lined the wagon road. He doffed his hat and wiped beads of sweat from his forehead before replacing it. The hat was an expensive one, as were all his clothes, from his fancy shirt and vest to his fawn pants and silver-chased riding boots. He sat in the saddle with the arrogance of a man accustomed to position but not with enough to irritate others.

His voice dropped a notch as he asked,

27

'What is this complaint Lindon was making?'

Nash lifted his hand and brought it down swiftly, as if to wipe Carr Lindon away. 'A man named Tindle has been trying to stir up a lynching party. I warned him but Lindon thinks I should stay around and see that he heeds the warning.'

'Lindon's afraid that Tyler won't come to trial, eh?' Griff murmured. 'If I were as good a friend of Tyler's as Lindon is, I might be afraid he *would* come to trial.'

Sheriff Nash turned his head slowly to study the solid man riding beside him. 'Meaning what by that?'

'There's a good deal of evidence against Tyler—that is, from what I hear there is.' Griff paused and then continued, 'If there were that much evidence against me, I'd be tempted to find a way to get out of standing trial.'

'I see,' Nash murmured and rode in silence until they had turned off the wagon road and gone the few hundred yards to where the T-Over ranch house sat solidly on its knoll, the outbuildings clustered behind and below it.

They left their horses and Nash walked ahead, stopping on the veranda and knocking loudly on the door. Griff remained in the yard, looking down at the soft dirt near where he stood. He motioned Finley over to his side.

'There've been riders here recently, Ed. They came fast and went fast.' He glanced up. Nash was still knocking, using the butt of his gun now, his cold features showing a hint of impatience.

'Open in the name of the law in there!'

Griff murmured. 'Go to the bunkhouse and see if they're in there, Ed. And tell Dutch and Perly to keep out of sight.'

Ed Finley lumbered away, disappearing around the corner as Nash's impatience got the better of him and he lifted the latch of the door. Griff hurried beside him as the door swung open. The big, cool parlor was empty.

A quick tour of the house was all that Nash needed. 'They left,' he said shortly.

Griff spread his hands. 'I'm sorry, Sheriff. But this afternoon they flatly refused to go. Apparently my threat to get you changed their minds.'

Finley came back, puffing a little from the exertion of having had to walk up the slope from the bunkhouse. He shut the door on the thickening twilight outside and Griff moved over to light one of the lamps. Finley said when he had his breath, 'Their stuff is gone. Looks like they've flown for good.'

'So it would seem,' Nash said dryly.

Griff looked about the room. 'I can't say that I'm displeased with my purchase. Tyler had a nice place here for a young man.' He shook his head. 'Again, I'm sorry, Sheriff. I wish you could have served the dispossess. I'd feel more legal that way.'

'It's legal enough.' Nash said shortly. 'And

29

I'll leave a call in town for Tyler's men to come see me. They'll be at the Buckhorn sooner or later.'

Finley coughed. Both men glanced at him. 'Is there any chance those three just made it look like they skipped and are waiting for the sheriff to leave? You know they threatened us today, Neil.'

Griff made a deprecatory motion with his hand, but Nash caught it up. 'With tempers running high over Tyler, it is possible,' he agreed.

Griff's laugh sounded a little nervous. 'What do you suggest, Sheriff?'

'They would go to Lindon's if they went anywhere,' he said. 'I'll ride by there on my way home. Otherwise, I suggest you keep an eye out until I've had a chance to talk with them.'

'But if they should attack?' Griff pressed.

Nash sounded reluctant. 'It is not illegal for a man to defend himself, Mr. Griff.' Nodding shortly, he settled his hat on his head and walked to the door. 'Good night.'

Griff stood listening until the hoofbeats of the sheriff's horse had faded. Then he laughed abruptly. 'Well, Ed?'

'I just hope it works,' Finley grumbled. He rubbed a heavy jowl with his fingers. 'You're putting too much weight on Tindle. The man isn't that capable.'

'I've thought of that,' Griff said. He strode

30

through to the kitchen. Opening the back door, he called, 'Dutch!' sharply.

In a moment a thick-barreled man came into the room, followed by a heavy-set blond one. Griff said to the first man, 'Nash is gone; get riding.'

Dutch grinned. 'Halfway there, Boss.'

He started away, followed by the blond man whose walk, from the rear, was surprisingly like that of Pat Tyler. 'Watch out for Lindon,' Griff warned. 'He's in town stewing about there may be a lynch party.'

'I'll handle him,' the blond man said.

'Let him alone, Perly. He's a good man to hang things on,' Griff ordered. His voice was sharp. 'Both of you. Your job is to get Nash. And don't hurry it. Wait until the mob is really acting. I want no slip-ups on this.'

'None,' Dutch agreed. 'I know my business, Boss.' He hesitated at the door. 'What if they got Tyler strung before Nash gets there?'

'They won't,' Griff said. 'Tindle will see to that. But if Tyler isn't out of that cell by the time you take care of Nash, see that he gets out—and rides.'

Dutch and Perly went out and soon the sounds of their horses going away at a fast pace faded into the swiftly darkening night. Griff turned to Finley, laughing softly. 'By the time Ogle and the rest of the town have this straightened around, Ed, we'll have things all our own way.'

31

Nash rode leisurely along the trail to the wagon road, across it, and then the quarter mile to Carr Lindon's L-in-C ranch. He was turning over in his mind what Griff had said and what he had left unsaid. Nash could not say that he liked the man. Nor could he say yet that he disliked him. Usually he was slow to form an opinion about another, concerning himself only with the man's standing before the law. A man was either within the law or he was without it. No middle ground existed for Sim Nash.

He did not like the way Griff had moved into Tyler's place. But the title was legal as far as he could see and he had to admit that a man would naturally be eager to get started on a new property with spring well along. Besides, it was not his place to question the ethics of Neil Griff's move, but simply to follow the legal procedures involved.

He drew rein as he broke into the open and looked at the dark hulk of the house ahead. Night had closed in completely now up here in the hills. There was no light, no sign of life from the place ahead. He rode forward slowly, mindful of Ed Finley's suggestion and wondering if the T-Over men would be touchy enough to buck him.

He sat in the yard between the house and

the outbuildings, but the only sounds he could make out were those of the animals in the barn and corral. Frowning, he was about to turn and retrace his route to the wagon road when he made out the faint beat of hoofs. They were coming from the west of him, he judged; a fair number of riders were causing them and going in the direction of the switchback trail.

It was Sim Nash's business to be suspicious of men and so his first thought was that there was something wrong with a group of men riding hard here at this time of night. He thought, Lindon has two men and Tyler has three; five men acting together could do a lot if they were led right.

He recalled Lindon's worry over Pat Tyler, his desire to have the man turned over to him until the danger to Tyler, if there was any, had passed. The fact that Nash discounted the danger did not make it any the less real to Carr Lindon, he knew. Nash swore softly. If L-in-C and T-Over men were trying to take advantage of his being away to free Tyler from jail . . .

Nash waited no longer, but headed his horse for the switchback road and pushed it as fast as he dared along the dark, unfamiliar trail.

*   *   *

The idea of taking Pat Tyler from jail was not a sudden one with Carr. Since his talk with

Nash, the beginnings of it had been in his mind. And when he saw Nash ride off with Neil Griff and Finley, he realized that there was no other course to follow. It was not just the ugly mood Ogle and the others in the saloon were working themselves into—although it was plain enough that Tindle was trying to work them up to lynch Tyler this night—it was the complete disregard that Nash had for the facts staring at him.

'He's too convinced of the strength of his own law,' Carr said aloud as he watched Peak and Ned Watts riding off. It was as if the sheriff thought the sound of the word 'law' itself was enough to maintain control.

Now Carr hurried toward the small house where Elsa lived, going this time by the front veranda. She came quickly in answer to his knock, opening the door wide and shutting it swiftly as he hurried in.

'Carr?'

He fought to keep the bitterness and anger from his voice. 'Nash just rode off with Griff.'

'I know,' she said. 'To serve that dispossess on T-Over.' She was silent a moment and then her eyes widened with realization. 'Carr—the lynch mob.'

'The lynch mob,' he said savagely. He stood in the center of the small parlor, turning his hat in his hands, wondering if he dared ask of her what he must. Finally he said, 'Elsa—I need that help you offered me.'

She was calm, standing tall and straight before him. 'Of course, Carr. I expected to give it.' She put a hand on his arm. 'But come into the kitchen and have some supper.'

'Thank you,' he said gravely. He followed her into the warmth of the kitchen and sat at the small table, watching her move about the room. She had the meal keeping warm on the stove and she served it, saying in laughing apology:

'If you don't mind eating Sim's dinner? He left in too much of a hurry.'

'A pleasure,' Carr said. He made no further reference to the matter until he had finished the meal and was taking his coffee. He watched her while he rolled a cigarette, and finally she lifted her eyes to his.

'There's nothing else you can do, is there, Carr?' She tipped the lamp-chimney and he bent, drawing up the flame to the end of his cigarette. 'You have to get Pat out.'

He showed his pleasure at her understanding. In rapid words, he sketched out the tentative plan he had made. She listened gravely, nodding now and then. When he was done, she spoke.

'Then as soon as you hear that Peak is here, you'll go.'

He rose and went around the table to her, and she stood to meet him. They faced each other silently for some time and then Carr lifted his hands and put them lightly on her shoulders. 'And when I go,' he said steadily, 'I go as a criminal.'

'Not in my eyes, Carr.'

'But in the eyes of the law, of the town. Could you stand thinking that of me?'

'It won't be what I think of you,' she said stubbornly.

'The pressure of public opinion,' he murmured.

'Carr! Carr, you fool. Do you think—'

He stopped her words with his lips, harshly, almost bruisingly. When he released her, he said, 'I wanted to hear that. But if you change your mind, I'll understand.'

The sound of someone running onto the front veranda and hammering on the door broke the reverie between them. With a questioning look at Carr, Elsa turned and hurried into the parlor. The hammering grew louder and a child's voice cried, 'Sheriff! Sheriff!'

Carr heard the door open. Elsa's voice was cool, still calm. 'Yes?'

'The sheriff, Miss Nash. Tell him to hurry. There's a mob gathering outside the jailhouse. Paw said to tell him—they look drunk and ugly, Miss Nash.'

'I'll tell him right away,' Elsa said. 'Thank you.' The door closed. Carr was at the rear door when she returned to the kitchen.

'No time,' he said bitterly. 'No time to wait for Peak.'

He loosened the gun in his holster. She said sharply, 'Wait, Carr. Sim has an extra set of keys in the house. I'll get them. And I'll get a horse ready for Pat.'

He turned this over quickly in his mind. It would be better, he thought. There might be a chance to do this quietly. If he had to blast the lock from the door with his gun, there was only a fifty-fifty chance of his getting Tyler out of the building, let alone free.

'I'll hold them if I can,' he said. 'Signal me when you've got Pat out.'

She watched him go, listened to his footsteps, harsh on the steps, softer on the dirt of the yard. 'And I too will be a criminal,' she murmured, and hurried away to find the keys.

Carr vaulted the low hedge that separated the yard from the alley and entered the jail by the rear door which opened to the annex of three cells that had been added with Sim Nash's coming to Buckhorn as sheriff. He saw a light in the center one and had a glimpse of Pat Tyler standing by his cot, looking inquiringly toward the door.

'Get ready, Pat. There's a mob forming.'

In the dim light from the small lamp, Pat Tyler's square face was haggard and drawn. But even so, he looked boyish with the one lock of heavy blond hair hanging down over his forehead. He said thickly, 'Ready, Carr.'

Carr went on, into the darkness of the office. He stopped long enough to light a lamp and then, deliberately, he threw open the door and stood there, framed by the light behind him.

A knot of men stood in the center of the street. Elsewhere it was deserted as if the townspeople not present had fled for safety. Carrs could make out Ogle and Purvis with Jerry Dyke on one side of them. Separated slightly from them were a number of others, the riffraff who hung around to do odd jobs when they needed money for liquor, a few from the hills. And standing in front of them all was the small, wiry Tindle.

It was Ogle who saw him first and his shout turned Tindle around. Pointing, the small man cried in his shrilly strong voice, 'I told you we couldn't wait. There's Lindon come to help the rustler!'

Carr said loudly, 'You reading my mind again?' He stood with one hand on his gun butt, his eyes fixed on the sullen crowd.

They aren't quite ready yet, he thought. They haven't worked themselves up as much as they need to. Ogle was carrying a long rope, noose-knotted at one end, and some of the men had pickaxes, but they were still just sullenly restless, not viciously so.

Carr thought with sour amusement as he watched Tindle hopping around, He wants to get it done before Nash comes back—and so do I. But it struck him that he might be able to hold them for a while, maybe long enough for

Peak to arrive and for Elsa to get the keys and free Pat from his cell.

'Get out of the way, Carr,' Ogle said thickly. He stood with the rope in his great red hands, swaying slightly. 'We're coming for Pat.'

'What are you waiting for?' Carr demanded. 'You know Nash won't be back for a while. Your friend Griff saw to that. There's no law to stop you now!'

'I care nothing for Nash or Griff,' Ogle said in his stubborn voice. 'If you don't want to get hurt, move out of the way.'

'I suppose you didn't know Nash was gone,' Carr taunted. 'You waited a long while then. What were you waiting for—Tindle to make up your minds?'

Ogle flushed and took a step forward, then stopped. 'It's not a thing a man likes to do,' he said.

'No,' Carr agreed. 'Killing your neighbor doesn't set well, does it?'

Ogle flinched as if he had been struck. There was a mutter through the crowd, silent up to now, watching Carr and Ogle as if the whole matter were a duel between them. Tindle said quickly, above the noise, 'A man ain't much of a neighbor when he steals from you and shoots at you.'

Carr looked steadily at him. 'If anything happens here, Tindle, you can count on my finding you and strangling you with that same rope.'

Tindle said something obscene but there was fear on his face and, in spite of himself, he backed toward Ogle and the front of the crowd.

Carr started down the steps, slowly. This was a tinder-dry situation, he knew, and it might explode any time. He could feel the temper of the mob, and he knew that he could hold it only a little longer. There was a chance that if he showed Tindle up for what he was, the others could be turned from the business.

Then Carr stopped on the second step, showing his disgust as Tindle wriggled through the front row and buried himself somewhere in the rear of the crowd. There was no reaction to this, only silence, a quiet, deadly waiting through which Carr could almost hear the hiss of an imaginary dynamite fuse. And he knew that they had finally made up their minds and nothing short of bullets would stop them now.

Behind him he heard a faint sound, a low voice. He did not move when Elsa said, 'All right, Carr.'

As if her words were a signal, a coyote yip came sharply through the night. Carr turned, jumping back for the door. From somewhere behind the jailhouse a gun went off, a man shouted a warning. The mob in front stood in momentary bewilderment and then broke at Tindle's warning cry:

'They're getting him out! Surround the jailhouse. Get Lindon!'

Carr turned, kicking the door shut behind him, and raced for the rear as a battering ram of bullets beat against the door where he had just been standing. He reached the annex and ran past the door of Tyler's empty cell and leaped into the darkness of the alley.

A gun flamed in the blackness. There was the sound of men running as those from the front of the jail swept around its sides. The boiling noise of men's voices was like the front of a great, incoming storm.

Carr stopped, pressed against the wall, waiting. Now he heard the beat of horses' hoofs leaving at full gallop. He started forward again to get free of the building before it was ringed by Tindle and the mob. He ran for the house and his own horse in Nash's yard. As he reached the hedge a voice cried from not five feet away:

'There's Lindon!'

A gun fired and dust spurted by Carr's feet. He went over the hedge, diving as another shot whipped the air above him. He lit rolling, feeling the air go from him at the jar which renewed the pain in his bruised body and jarred his yet unhealed ribs. He rolled back against the hedge, fighting for breath as he lay still listening to the men running past, shouting to one another.

A sudden patch of light came from Elsa's kitchen as the door was opened briefly. The light disappeared almost immediately, but it gave Carr a chance to see that his horse was there, not ten feet away, by the corner of the bar. He thanked Elsa silently and stood, then made a dash for the animal. Freeing the reins, he lifted a foot to the stirrup.

From behind him, the sheriff's familiar voice said coldly, 'That's far enough, Lindon.'

Carr took his foot from the stirrup and turned in the darkness. He said softly, 'What crime have I committed, Sheriff?'

'We'll talk of that later.' Nash came toward him, only a shape in the blackness. The moon was high enough to throw a faint light through the trees shading the yard and a bit of it filtered onto the gun he held in his hand, showing Carr how unwaveringly it pointed toward his midriff.

'I'm under arrest for trying to protect your jail for you!'

'I'm the law here. I do my own protecting.'

Carr knew that he was wasting time again in argument. Nash had one idea in his mind and one idea only. And soon one of the running, shouting remains of the mob that was still seeking him would think to get a torch and he would be seen.

He said, 'Let's go then. But I hope you do a better job of feeding your prisoners than you do of protecting them.'

It was unfair, Carr knew, to say what he had. Nash was scrupulously honest and untiring when it came to working for the law. But his

42

words did what Carr hoped they would—they broke through Nash's cold hard shell momentarily. For an instant his anger bested his control, and he took a threatening step forward.

Carr was waiting, poised on the balls of his feet. He went to meet Nash, moving slightly sideways as he did so. His arm came up, driving against Nash's wrist, knocking his gun arm sideways. With the force of his turn, Carr drove his fist sharply into the sheriff's face. Nash went backward, silently, not stumbling, and simply stretched himself onto the ground.

Amazed at the ease of his victory, Carr stood still a moment, looking down at the man. Now he could hear sounds of pursuit—some still close, others distant as riders headed out of town. But, in the darkness of the yard, it had grown still again. Carr knelt carefully by the sheriff, making sure that there was no trickery. Nash lay where he had fallen, his gun beside one limp hand, his breathing ragged and shallow.

Thrusting the sheriff's gun back into its holster, Carr bent and strained upward, lifting the man, and carried him toward his house. Nash was light for a person of his height but even so Carr felt the weakness from his days in bed and he was staggering by the time he reached the door. His footsteps brought a sound from the other side, an inquiry out of the darkness.

He called out carefully, 'Elsa?'

'Carr! What are you doing here?'

'Let me in. Your brother is here—hurt.'

The door opened and he walked into the darkness. In a moment she opened the door leading to the parlor and the light from there guided him. Elsa took part of the burden and together they stretched Nash onto the sofa. Carr brought the lamp closer and took a careful look at the unconscious man. The blow he had landed had been flush on the jaw. It accounted for the bruise beginning to form but it could not account for the fresh blood Carr found on the hand that had rested against the sheriff's back.

'He's been shot,' Carr said in a puzzled voice. 'That's why he went down so easy.'

She hesitated only briefly. Then she moved closer to Carr. 'Ride, please,' she pleaded. 'Go after Pat and the others before it's too late.'

'In a minute.' He was peeling off Nash's coat and shirt.

'I'll get Doctor Mason for Sim, Carr,' she said. 'Now hurry.'

Carr nodded and continued working. He said as he slipped the limp arm through the shirt sleeve, 'If you see Bette Mason, Elsa— tell her that Pat is going to be all right.'

She said hopelessly, 'Must you always concern yourself with other people?'

He did not answer. He had found the wound. It was high in the shoulder, with two

44

holes to show where the bullet had gone in at the rear and come out in front. He let a breath of relief run out of him. 'Not much,' he said. 'He's lost a lot of blood, that's about all. He'll be all right after the Doc patches him up—'

'Carr . . . !' Her voice was tense with warning.

He could hear the sounds of footsteps on the front porch now. Straightening up, he went quickly toward the kitchen, blowing out the lamp and setting it down as he did so. He swung open the back door. The thin light of the moon came slanting down, striking squarely into the face of a man moving, catlike, toward him. It was Mort Ogle and his gun was drawn.

Carr did not pause. He kept on going—there was nothing else to do. He and Ogle met on the low back steps. Ogle's gun was steady, hard against Carr's middle.

'Shoot and then finish off the sheriff,' Carr said. 'You only hit him in the shoulder.'

'Just put your hands up, Carr.' There was a stubborn weariness in Ogle's voice. But he did sound completely sober.

'Are you afraid to shoot a man from the front, Mort? Do you have to aim at the back like you did with Nash?'

Ogle's gun dug deeper, and Carr heard the click of the hammer as it went back. Ogle's hoarse breathing was loud in his ears, and he could feel hatred coming from the man.

45

He said, 'You can't do it, Mort,' and swung his flat with all the strength he had. At the same time he went sideways, falling away. He saw Ogle's look of surprise and heard the grunt of pain as his blow landed.

Ogle went off balance. Carr recovered himself and lashed out with his foot, driving Ogle's gun arm upward. The gun went off this time, booming its deep sound through the air, sending a lance of flame hurling up into the night. Carr was on the man, slashing with both fists and then running over Ogle as he fell. Carr reached and got the gun from him and jerked it free. He flung it across the yard as he found his horse and leaped into the saddle.

Ogle shouted from where he was struggling to rise, 'There goes Lindon!'

Carr reined around as someone with a lighted lamp opened the door, spilling light out onto Ogle. It was Tindle and he held a lamp in one hand and his gun in the other. Behind him Elsa Nash came running. She grabbed his gun arm and Tindle flung it backward, deliberately hitting her with his elbow, knocking her back into the kitchen.

Carr held his horse still with a savage twist of the reins. He drew his own gun, took careful aim, and fired.

The last sound he heard from Tindle was a bubbling shriek as the bullet took him in the arm, shattering it. Carr holstered his gun, swung about, and drove his horse up the alley and away from town.

CHAPTER FOUR

Pat Tyler asked no questions when Elsa Nash came to his cell door with the key. Carr's brief words had left him no need for questions.

'Peak and Ned are waiting by my barn with a horse,' she said. 'Your men are up the street.'

Tyler said, 'Thanks to you—and Carr.' As the door swung quietly open, he stepped out, hesitating.

'Go on,' she said hurriedly. When he still did not move, she added, 'I'll talk to Bette. She believes in you, Pat.'

'Thanks,' he said, and turned to go. Once more he stopped. 'And you—how do you get out of here?'

'The sheriff's sister is safe enough,' she said. 'Go now.'

Tyler found the men and the horse waiting impatiently. He mounted and they started out quietly, going down the alley that ran in front of the small barn, heading northward. Someone appeared at the upper end of it, coming rapidly toward them. When it was too late to turn, Tyler saw that it was Sim Nash.

'Ride him down!' old Peak shrilled, spurring his horse forward to hit Nash's animal with the

47

shoulder of his own. Nash's gun flamed crazily upward as he went off balance. Another shot blended with his, sounding almost as if it were the same one. Then the riders had swept past, beating away in the darkness. Another figure on horseback seemed to be at the distant mouth of the alley, but Tyler could not be sure in the darkness, and when they reached the end, there was no one in sight.

The three rode in silence, turning eastward when they left the alley, and picking up the T-Over men waiting as they had been told to. They all pressed their horses now, forcing them up thin, worn tracks that cut between the switchbacks until they were on the bench above town. There, in the timber, they reined in to let their tired animals blow.

'We hit for the high country,' old Peak said.

'We'll wait for Carr,' Tyler told them. 'Or I will. You ride on.'

'You go plumb to hell,' Peak said indignantly.

'Plumb,' Ned Watts echoed.

'Besides,' Peak said, 'Carr didn't risk his hide to get you caught again.'

'I'm waiting,' Pat Tyler said stubbornly. 'We're safe enough here until daylight.' He looked through the darkness at his three hands who had been silent up to now. 'There was no call for you to mix in on this.'

Milo Carter said in his truculent way, 'No call for us to stay out, neither. I don't like being pushed around no more'n you do.'

Rick Bettle, solid and blocky in the darkness, cleared his throat and spat. 'Maybe you done it like they say. I wouldn't know. But I figure if you did, you had a reason.'

Old Bill Marcus, the youngest of the three, was a scarecrow of a man with hair so white that it showed that way a little even at night. He moved his horse to get closer to Tyler. 'When we came out here with your dad, we didn't wear our guns just to look pretty, Pat. They ain't just for show now.'

'All right,' Tyler said. 'Thanks.' He let it lie; there wasn't much more a man could say at a time like this.

They sat and waited, talking in low tones; now and then stopping to listen to faint sounds from below. The moonlight grew stronger and they were able to see as well as hear the small squad of men coming. They had started up the switchback, moving steadily, but slowly, following each loop in the trail rather than cutting across them. The six at the top drew deeper into the timber. They were silent now.

As the riders neared, Tyler heard Jerry Dykes say, 'Ogle's crazy. I say they'll head for the west breaks, not the valley.'

'They could make it faster by way of the valley,' Purvis argued.

Dyke said, 'Let's split then. I'll take the breaks. You go through the valley.'

They stopped briefly at the top to rest their

horses and discuss their routes. There were six of them and they broke into threes. A short way up there was a fork in the trail, marked by a clump of firs, and here they took different routes. The men headed by Jerry Dyke went straight ahead toward the west breaks. Purvis took his group to the right, along the trail that would lead onto Carr's land and so to the wagon road and the valley.

When the sounds of their going had faded completely, old Peak swore sourly. 'Hear that?' he demanded 'They do it that way and we're cut off proper from the high country.'

'Can't go down nor up,' Ned Watts said in a tone of finality.

There was silence for a moment while each man considered this predicament. Finally Pat Tyler said, 'There's the way around by the east, back of my place. It's rough and we can't make the last pitch until daylight, but if the snow doesn't lay too deep up above yet, we can make it.'

'Griff is on T-Over,' Ned Watts said.

Milo Carter started to swear and Pat Tyler cut him off short. 'Griff is on T-Over?'

'Since today,' old Peak told him. 'After beating Carr and recovering himself a mite, he showed up with title to your place and asked Nash for a dispossess. He got it and today he moved up there.'

Milo Carter swore again and Tyler let him wear it out. Milo said finally, 'They come up big as life this afternoon, him and Finley, waving a danged paper at me. We run 'em off, me and the boys. They said they'd see about it and didn't put up no fight nor nothing. Just rode off.'

'Sure, to get the sheriff,' Peak said disgustedly. 'Carr sent me and Ned up to haul these three away, Pat, before they started shooting up the law and making matters worse.' He cackled as if that were a joke. 'If they could be worse.'

Tyler was puzzled. 'Griff didn't need the law. He has enough men to run us all off our places if he wants. Gun slingers. I saw some of them.'

Peak spat. 'Like Carr says, it was smart getting the sheriff to do his work for him. Makes him law-abiding, don't it? And it got Nash out of the way for Tindle and his mob too.'

It was Tyler who did the swearing this time. 'Nash knows all this—and he still won't believe me.' He fell silent, nursing the realization bitterly. He was usually an exuberant man, one who took life as it came and enjoyed it as best he might. But since his return from Spokane Falls the week before, he had been silent, on the verge of such bitterness as he now felt. And at this moment it flooded him, threatening to choke him.

Finally he said, 'We'll wait for Carr to warn him they're ahead.'

It was accepted without comment and they continued to sit where they were, feeling the cold of the hills beginning to lift from the ground and creep into them. Now and then one of the horses would stir, but for the most part they were as quiet as the men.

At last there was the sound of a lone rider coming fast through the deep stillness of the night. Tyler eased his horse to a position where he could see the trail more easily. When the rider was close, Tyler eased out the gun Peak had brought for him.

Then the man rode through a patch of moonlight, his horse lathered and straining. Tyler let the gun drop back into its holster.

'Carr!'

Carr drew his horse in, hesitating. Tyler spoke again and Carr turned into the timber. His mount stood with its legs splayed a little, head hanging from weariness at the rough climb below. Tyler told him briefly of the six who had gone by.

Carr considered this. Then he said, 'We'll have to ride through Griff and go up the east trail. It's a chance but there's no other way.'

'Fight through Dyke or Purvis,' Ned Watts said hopefully.

'Jerry Dyke is still a neighbor,' Carr reminded him. 'And so is Purvis. I had to hit Ogle tonight and I shot Tindle. Tindle is scum, but I can't shoot Ogle or Purvis or Dyke—not yet.'

'Nor I,' Pat Tyler agreed somberly.

Carr said, in a dry voice, 'One of the charges against you is that you shot at them the other day.'

'The other day,' Pat Tyler said, 'I was in a cabin in the high country being guarded by one of Neil Griff's men.'

'Ah, the story you told the sheriff. What was it all about, Pat?'

'A waste of breath as far as Nash was concerned,' Tyler said. He rolled a cigarette with stiff fingers and let it hang unlighted between his lips. The tobacco seemed to give him some comfort even if he dared not smoke it. 'I went to see you in the hospital the day before you got out. You were still asleep, so I called on Bette and then rode home after dark. Griff was waiting for me on the trail and—'

'Couldn't you have shot him?' Peak asked curiously.

'In cold blood?' Tyler demanded.

'Go on, Pat,' Carr said with quiet understanding.

Tyler rumpled the cold cigarette in his fingers and held it. 'He told me we were going to push thirty head up the Trail that night and twenty the next day. He even gave me a hand.' He spoke mechanically now, as if he had said this before. 'We did, shoving them into the Bowl. There was a campfire there and two men around it—Griff called them Perly and

Dutch. Perly was a big blond about my size.'

'Oh,' Carr said, seeing how neatly Griff had done things.

'That's right,' Tyler said. 'Griff threw down on me. I tried to take him but the one called Dutch got in a lick with his gun barrel and knocked me down. Griff had them take my hat and vest and then rope me. Dutch hauled me up the ridge behind the Bowl to that old cabin there and kept me all night and until afternoon. Then he rode me to here, cut the ropes, and told me to head for town.

'By then,' Tyler said, 'I had an idea of what Griff had planned, so I went to Nash. He was gone—with Ogle and the others, I learned later—so I sat and talked with Elsa until he came.' The bitterness returned to his voice. 'She told me to ride, but I'd had enough of it. How was I to know he wouldn't listen?' He mimicked Nash's cold tones savagely. ' "The word of a confessed rustler means nothing, Tyler." ' He took a deep, steady breath. 'And, by God, he's let Griff ride free while I rotted in his jailhouse.'

'According to him, he's thinking about it,' Carr said. He made a sharp gesture with his hand. 'He's storing it up, Pat. He's no fool. The only thing is—how long will it be before he gets enough stored for some of it to start soaking in?'

'Too long,' Ned Watts said.

'So I know,' Carr said in soft agreement. He

54

patted his horse. 'We're ready now. Let's ride.'

They took the trail Larry Purvis had taken, cutting off to follow a low ridge that would drop them down a steep pitch directly onto the Saddle that Griff now controlled. This was Carr's land, but they went across it as carefully as if it were patrolled by the enemy. Before they reached the drop to the Saddle, Carr stopped the others, left his horse, and walked to a vantage point where he could look down. The moon was fat now, nearing fullness, and the light of it on the open trail was clear and cold. He could see riders strung out on the wagon road.

He walked back and joined the others. 'They're coming along down there,' he said. 'To look at my place I suppose. It blocks us from the valley and T-Over.'

'Once daylight comes and they can track, they can't miss us,' Tyler said.

The moon that had been a help was now a definite hindrance. Under its radiance, the spread of land below was clear and sharply outlined. Carr realized that without deep darkness they had no chance to try any of the possible routes. They could only wait and hope the scouting parties would withdraw soon.

Carr said, 'Peak, you and Ned go back to the place. If you can get into the bunkhouse in time, you might claim you know nothing about this.'

'The sheriff knows I was in on it,' Peak said.

55

'I yelled at him.'

'Old fool talks too much,' Ned Watts said.

Carr was silent, working this over in his mind. Then he said, 'Milo, maybe you and the boys can do it.'

'T-Over goes with Pat,' Milo Carter answered.

'Damn it, we'll need someone on my place—both to keep an eye on what's happening and to bring us supplies if we're up there for any length of time.'

'Do it that way, boys,' Tyler said.

It was obviously an order, and after a few minutes taken out to grumble and settle exactly what was to be done, Milo and the two other T-Over men turned their horses and worked back through the rough land and out of sight. The group remaining fell silent.

It grew colder now and occasionally a man would shift his position, moving about to take the stiffness from his muscles. Carr slipped away again, finding a fold of rock where he could lie and watch the Saddle below. A man had been posted there as a guard by the scouting riders and he rode back and forth across the wide road. Whether he was one of Purvis' men or had been put there by Griff, Carr could not know.

Shortly, Tyler joined him, squatting alongside, his expression bleak under the harsh light of the moon. Carr waited and, when he didn't speak, said quietly, 'I've been trying to get you to explain all your strange activities for a week now, Pat. It's about time, isn't it?'

'About,' Pat Tyler agreed. He spoke in a low voice, detailing to Carr the whole story. Carr listened in silence, not surprised to see how close he had come to judging Griff as the backbone of the present trouble. A man like Griff, he thought, would act to a pattern. He had seen a piece of that pattern almost worked against himself. It wasn't hard to picture the whole of it fitting a man with Pat Tyler's temperament.

Tyler said. 'I was suckered, that's all, Carr. It started with Finley coming here and buying all that worthless land like he did. The money Finley used is Griff's, by the way. And if you'll take a map and plat out the land they have, you'll see that the five of us who run beef in the valley are almost surrounded.

'While Finley was doing this,' Pat went on in the same low voice, 'Finley looked over those who might be useful to them. He picked me.'

'Why?'

Tyler grimaced. 'The way Griff talks, it's because I'm impulsive. And I'll gamble. And when I get in a corner, I lose my head. Maybe he's right. I don't usually think too much before I do something.' He spoke like a man who has had time to look into himself, and what he had seen he did not like too well.

'Not much,' Carr agreed quietly.

'Then,' Tyler said, 'I got to talking about wanting new breeding stock for my horse herd and Finley took advantage of that. You remember, Finley got a dodger in his mail and passed it on to me. Well, he wrote Griff in Spokane Falls, had him make the dodger up and I fell for it.'

'Any of us would have,' Carr said. 'Remember, Ogle nearly went with you to that sale.'

'How many would have been taken in so easily, though? Oh, there was a sale all right. That's where I picked up the splay-footed horse and some others. But I didn't even suspect anything when I met Finley there. And, well, a man in a strange town is apt to welcome a familiar face—even Ed Finley's. He introduced me to Griff after the sale and it ended up with my getting into a card game with them. I got taken, Carr.'

'Too much whiskey?'

'That and not enough caution. They played me like they tried to play you? I won most of the hands the first night and Griff was just as careful to throw in his hand and give me the pot as he was the night he tried to ring you. Only I fell for it.'

He was silent a moment, re-living it, and Carr said, 'Go on, fellow. Get it out.'

Tyler shrugged. 'The next day I thought I'd push my luck and we finished up the game. They squeezed me and I lost. I lost

T-Over, everything. Then Griff made me his proposition. I was to push some beef out of the valley. He even swore it would be put back after he consolidated his position. He made it sound good, as though he was coming in to make something of the worthless land he bought, and that he wanted no more of the valley than his share. But he thought that if he kept you and the others occupied with chasing your beef that disappeared from the valley, you'd be too busy to try to close in against him.'

'Why would we—if he was just planning what he said?'

'You wouldn't,' Tyler agreed softly. 'But I was fighting for my land—maybe that's why I believed him. Maybe I didn't want to believe anything else. Damn it, Carr, I don't know! But I fell for it, and by the time I saw what was really happening, it was too late.'

'Griff is smart, and he can make a man like him when he wants to. It could have happened to any of us, Pat.'

Tyler was silent a moment, and even his silence was bitter. Finally he said, 'He's smart all right. He's pushing his way in here the easy way. By the time Ogle and the rest get through running in circles after us, Griff will be in. It's easier to hold a man off from the outside than get him out once he's in. There can be a bloody war, Carr.'

'I know,' Carr agreed. 'When Griff took

59

over your place, he got control of the Saddle. I can't make Ogle see that if he wants to force the rest of us out, he can do so. How much beef could we run in and out if we had to haul it all up and down the rimrock that circles most of the valley? But Ogle can't see it. He can't see anything but the fact you took his beef.'

Tyler swore without heat, listlessly, as if Ogle had lost his importance now. He said, 'How will Griff do it? That's what I don't know yet.'

'My guess,' Carr said thoughtfully, 'is that he won't tell us to get off until he's forced to. The way he's played it so far shows that he wants to keep on the side of the law if he can. He'll just put his beef in the valley and let them push us out.'

'I messed things up good, didn't I?' Tyler said.

Carr didn't answer, except to say, 'It still doesn't explain why Griff tried to play me that night in the saloon.'

'Finley would have warned Griff that you were the one to watch out for,' Tyler said. 'That you were my friend—only I didn't have enough sense to realize it when you tried to help me the other day.'

Carr lay still, listening to the sounds of men in the near distance, combing the land on both sides of the wagon road. The guard below continued to ride back and forth, stopping now to beat his arms across his chest because of the cold. The portion of the valley Carr could see lay bathed in moonlight, a great silver and black bowl, stretching northward from the foot of the Saddle, enclosed east and west by sheer rimrock, and opening on the north only onto the rough, broad slash through the timber that was Rustler's Trail.

The Trail had been named, Carr thought, before he came. And since his time the name had had none of its true meaning. Except for a flurry of lawlessness caused by the inrush of gold miners the year before, this land had been at peace. Until now, he added in his mind. Until the coming of Neil Griff.

He became aware of Tyler's bitter silence again and he said, 'Sometimes, Pat, a man does a cockeyed thing. He knows it's wrong because it goes against his grain. And he shows that. You've been showing it ever since you brought those horses back from Spokane Falls. But it's done.'

'Sometimes there's an undoing,' Pat Tyler said.

'At times. In this case, Griff would have come in by force if he couldn't get in any other way. He may have to—yet. What Griff would have done—what Griff will do—didn't bear on your actions. Remember that. The way Griff decided to do it is what you got mixed up in.'

'Putting it that way makes me feel some better,' Tyler said.

'Take the weight off your mind. You've got other things to put on it,' Carr told him. 'Ogle has to be warned somehow. So do the others. So does Nash. Once Griff gets rolling he's going to be hard to stop.'

Pat Tyler made a harsh sound. 'What makes you think there'll be a chance they'll listen?'

'I don't,' Carr said. 'They probably won't listen until it's too late. Most men don't.'

CHAPTER FIVE

Neill Griff sat before the fireplace, his feet extended to the crackling fire, and listened to the sounds of trackers coming closer and then fading. He looked at Finley, seated farther from the fire, and lifted his whiskey glass.

'To all worriers, Ed—like yourself.' He laughed, a deep, rich sound. 'It's falling into place perfectly; stop being so edgy.'

Finley cocked his head, listening. 'I wish Dutch and Perly would get back,' he said. 'What if it's them they're tracking?'

'We'd have heard about it by now,' Griff said. He sipped his drink contentedly. 'They'll be back. Probably they're trying to get through this crew now.'

Finley continued to look worried. He said finally, 'Neil, we've made a good thing of this so far. It's worked out exactly as you planned it. But where do we go from here?'

'Why,' Griff murmured, 'we let these cow farmers wear themselves out hunting for Tyler and maybe Lindon, if he's fool enough to go on like he is. Then we make the big drive. We run our cattle in and set it up so they have to move theirs out. Then the valley is ours, Government graze or not; it will belong to the Leaning-G. And it's legal enough. By the time "I'm-the-Law" Nash wakes up—if he lives to wake up—it will take the U. S. Cavalry to move us.'

'And from there?' Finley insisted.

'From there onto the Bunchgrass graze. From there to controlling this country, Ed. In Texas they have ranches big enough to swallow this Territory. We'll have us a ranch like they have in Texas.'

Finley said with admiration in his voice, 'If you don't get it one way, you take it another.'

'So I do,' Griff agreed. 'But force is just the final resort of a smart man, Ed. Don't show it until you have to. Then it has that much more power in it.'

Finley seemed about to ask another question when the sound of footsteps came from the rear veranda. Griff was on his feet in one easy motion, one hand on his hip near the gun at his belt. The kitchen door opened and Dutch and Perly came in.

Dutch wiped imaginary sweat from his face. 'Them crazy fools are plumb wild, Boss.

They're liable to shoot anything that moves tonight.'

Griff waved both men to a chair. Dutch stretched out, grinning as if pleased with himself. Perly sat and glared at the fire.

'Damn it,' Griff said. 'Give us the news. What happened—is it Tyler or Lindon or you they're hunting?'

Dutch turned his head indolently. He rolled a cigarette with deliberate slowness, keeping one eye on Griff, measuring the limit of the man's patience.

'Me and Perly picked Nash up going hell bent for town on the switchback.' He laughed gustily. 'He was chasing after Lindon's and Tyler's crews, I think. Anyway, we were right behind him but he was too busy to notice. And it was like they knew we were coming. Lindon and his men broke Tyler out of jail just as Nash headed down the alley that goes alongside his barn.' He laughed again. 'There they came, that fool Peak heading 'em and yelling so Nash could make sure who it was. Nash pulled his gun and when it went off, mine did too. Then Perly and me faded to see the fun. The shots started the mob out front of the jailhouse and they were shooting and banging at anything that moved for a while.'

'Well, what about Nash?'

Dutch made a face. 'I guess it was a mite too dark. I got him in the shoulder from what I heard later. He's down but he ain't out by a long way.' His laugh came again. 'But it ain't so bad, because it seems that Lindon didn't ride with Tyler and the bunch. Nash caught him in his yard and got the drop on him. Lindon knocked him down. The last I heard, Nash was convinced Lindon put up one of his men to doing the shooting. Or he thinks it was Tyler. It looks to me like it don't matter much.'

'Good,' Griff said. 'Better than if you'd hit him square in the brisket, Dutch.' He nodded in satisfaction, 'So then, the mob is chasing Tyler?'

'Some of 'em rode after him. Others were chasing their own tails around the town.'

'And what happened to Lindon?'

Dutch frowned. 'You got to watch for that Lindon, Boss. They trapped him in Nash's house and he ran out, right over Ogle holding a gun on him, shot Tindle's arm half off, and got loose.'

'He's no man's fool,' Finley said warningly. He rose and brought a bottle and glasses and poured drinks for Dutch and Perly. 'I guess they earned a shot.'

Griff was looking thoughtfully into the fire. 'Maybe it isn't smart to wait for Ogle or Nash to get rid of Lindon for me. Maybe we ought to see to it sooner?'

'That,' Finley said, 'is worth drinking to.'

*   *   *

The first faint hint of dawn made a line of half-light over the eastern mountains. Below where Carr lay, the guard was still patrolling.

The sound of hurried footsteps scraping on rock came from behind him and he got stiffly to his feet, crouched now in darkness as the moon had slid low toward the west.

'Carr!' It was a husky whisper, an old man's excited voice.

Carr felt Pat Tyler, who had been dozing, come awake beside him. Putting out an arm to guide Tyler, Carr moved toward the voice. It was Peak and he was breathing hard as if he had been running.

'There's a half dozen coming from the west,' he said. 'They're moving slow, following our tracks with a lantern.'

'They didn't wait until daylight,' Tyler said bitterly. He turned hopelessly to Carr.

'Where's Ned?' Carr said.

'Bringing the horses.' Peak took a deep breath. 'Ride 'em down, I say. When a man acts like Ogle's been acting, he ain't my neighbor no more.'

'We'll ride,' Carr said calmly. 'But there'll be no shooting—not to hit a man.' He heard the horses coming, and eased through the dark toward them. When they were mounted, he added, 'We'll go quietly and when we get as close as we can, I'll put a shot into the air. Maybe surprise will break us through.'

'And then?' Tyler asked.

'Then scatter. We'll meet in the high country. You know that piece of canyon east of the Bowl.' He reined his horse around. 'And if you have to shoot, shoot plenty high. I want no man saying we tried to kill our neighbors.'

They moved slowly through darkness, following Carr, whose knowledge of this land enabled him to keep on the narrow, rough trail. He broke over a rise, onto a small, half-timbered flat, and stopped. Below he could see the dim, bobbing light of a lantern. It took a few moments for his eyes to adjust and then he was able to make out a crew of riders bunched around one man on foot. He held the lantern and when he straightened up and pointed, Carr knew their tracks had been located again.

'Now,' he said softly. Drawing his gun, he sent a single shot blasting upward. His heels raked against the horse's flanks and he went forward, down the slope toward the men on the flat.

Old Peak let out a yell like a charging Indian. Behind Carr, two guns roared. Carr saw the lantern make a crazy bobbing as the man holding it leaped into the saddle. Then the bunched crew broke apart and one of them shouted, 'It's Carr and Tyler.'

He recognized the voice of Jerry Dyke. That meant he had left off combing the west brakes and had come back south, picking up three extra men from somewhere. Carr felt a faint thread of hope run through him. Now, at least, if they broke out of here, they wouldn't have to worry about running into another crew to the west.

The six on the flat started to regroup, forming a line. Carr fired his gun again, and the man with the lantern threw his light to the ground, and darkness closed down again. Now there was no sound beyond the beating of hoofs and the sudden rising crescendo of gunfire.

Almost alongside Carr, Tyler said, 'They aren't shooting in in the air!'

Carr heard the whisper of a bullet not far above his head. 'Keep low and ride!'

Peak whooped again and as he hit the flat, and had room to maneuver, came alongside Carr and Tyler. Ned Watts rode closely behind, his stubby body tight in the saddle. Carr saw a blob in the dark and then it disappeared. A gun blasted almost in his face, sending his horse sideways with fright.

He jerked the reins savagely, felt his horse strike something that gave way. A man cried out. Carr lashed at a dim face before him, saw it dissolve as his gun barrel raked against flesh. Then he was through, past the line, and the sounds of shooting were behind him. He drove his horse on to the edge of the flat and swung off the trail into the edge of timber.

He could hear horses and men, neighs and shouting, but there was no more shooting as the scattered crew under Dyke obviously feared hitting one another.

A rider came thundering toward Carr and went past. He recognized Pat Tyler. Then old Peak, swearing softly and steadily, with Ned Watts at his heels, swept by. Carr stayed where he was, listening as men raced without direction, chasing one another, confused by the dark that made everyone equal.

One came on toward Carr. He waited and then, when the rider was nearly to him, moved onto the trail. 'Hold it!'

The man sawed the reins and his horse reared, front feet pawing the air. It settled back and the rider swore harshly.

It was Jerry Dyke. Carr said, 'Stay where you are. You've made enough of a fool of yourself for one night.'

'By God, Carr . . .' Dyke sounded almost as if he would cry from the helplessness of his rage.

Carr said, 'We could have shot you all, packed there on the flat like a herd of beef. Remember that when you start thinking things over. And remember, too, that we shot into the air.'

'I don't shoot to miss,' Dyke told him.

'So I know now,' Carr said. Without warning, he sent his horse forward, angled it alongside Dyke, and slashed down at the man's head with the butt of his gun. A half-raised cry died in Dyke's throat as he lifted out of the saddle, went sideways, and rolled limply along the rough ground.

Carr took a moment to climb down, push Dyke to a safer spot off the trail and tie his horse. Then he mounted again and rode on, hurrying to catch the others.

*　　　*　　　*

Elsa Nash bent over her brother and listened to his rough breathing. Then, gently, she laid a hand on his thin cheek to test the amount of fever there. It was down, she told herself, and straightening, she slipped quietly from the room.

She moved about her day's chores with a calm efficiency that hid the anguish inside her. Now and then she would stop to look in on Nash and each time he seemed to be breathing easier, resting more calmly. According to Doctor Mason, he was in no great danger—the wound was clean and his body strong—and outside of deep pity, she did not think of Nash except mechanically. It was to Carr that her mind turned. Night had gone and the day was half over and there had been no word.

Perhaps it was as well, she thought. There could be news she would dread to hear. With each sound of men riding into town to seek rest or to be replaced by others, she would stand and listen, waiting for one to stop before the sheriff's house and bring the information that Carr had been found. A few came to the door, mostly townspeople, and each time only to inquire after Nash. Her answer was always the same:

'He's resting quietly, thank you.'

Finally, in the early part of the afternoon, it was Ogle who came, his heavy face drawn from lack of sleep, his eyes great holes of weariness. He stood on the veranda, stolidly, his hat twisting in his hands.

She gave him the same answer she had given the others and he said, 'When he wakes, tell him we'll get them for him, Miss Elsa.'

She looked steadily at him, making no effort to hide the contempt she felt. 'I'm not sure he'd want you to be the one to do it, Mr. Ogle.'

He winced as if she had struck him, but none of the set stubborness went from his face. 'If a man shot me, I'd want him found. I wouldn't care who did it.'

'What makes you think Carr shot him?' She kept her voice level with an effort. She was a strong woman, a steady woman as a rule, but of late she had found it hard to maintain her calm in the face of some of the things she had seen and heard.

'Shot him or had him shot,' Ogle said. 'Nash said so.'

'Sim said Carr knocked him down,' she answered. 'That's a different thing, Mr. Ogle. Carr knocked him down and found he was hurt and brought him inside to tend him. He risked his own life to do it.'

71

'Ah-h,' Ogle said, as if arguing with a woman in love—or any woman—was only a waste of breath.

Elsa went on, letting free some of the things that had been stored inside her, 'Carr has risked his life and his life's work for friendship, too, Mr. Ogle. What have you put up against yours?' Her voice continued cool and level although she found it necessary to cling to the edge of the door to hide the shaking of her body.

Ogle looked at her without comprehension. 'I'm fighting for my land,' he said. His voice was almost puzzled, as if this was something she should know. 'I'm chasing a cattle rustler and his—his . . .'

'Accomplice, Mr. Ogle?'

Ogle nodded, not speaking. She said, 'You've known Carr Lindon since he came here as a boy, haven't you? Fourteen years. And you've known Pat Tyler longer. And you can say that about them.'

'I saw the evidence,' Ogle said. Before the contempt in her eyes, he was almost defensive. Had she shouted at him or cried or done any of the things a woman was supposed to do, he would have known how to answer. But this reached deep through the wall of his weariness and where it touched it hurt somehow.

'You saw the evidence you were supposed to see,' she answered. 'You're blind, just as Sim is blind. And even if you found yourself wrong, you're too stubborn to turn back now.' Her knuckles where she gripped the door were white with the effort of holding herself in.

'Are you so small that you can listen to a man like Tindle and turn your back on Carr?'

Ogle was silent. His hands were still now, no longer twisting his hat. His face was without expression. His eyes showed nothing but his weariness.

'I'll tell Sim what you said, Mr. Ogle.' She moved to close the door.

Ogle licked his lips. 'You better tell him what you said,' he answered surprisingly. 'You better tell him so he'll know why we have to watch you too.' He turned and walked heavily away, leaving her nothing to do but shut the door and lean against it for support. It crossed her mind that if she were a man she could curse him or fight him. And then she shook her head, smiling humorlessly at herself. What good would that do? What good would anything do against the walls of preconceived prejudice men like Mort Ogle built to shield their minds?

'Know the truth and it shall make you free,' she murmured.

She turned from the door and went quietly in to see how her brother was. He still slept and she left the room.

*   *   *

Darkness had come and there was still no news of Carr. She had noticed that there had been fewer groups of riders coming and going, less stir through the town. And she wondered if they were tiring of this or if Carr had been found and no one had thought to come with the news. Or, she added to herself, if Ogle had told them not to come with the news—to her.

Shortly after her brief supper, Doctor Mason came to see Nash. His daughter Bette was with him and the sight of her reminded Elsa that she had forgotten her promise to Pat Tyler.

Mason was a solid man, beefy now with middle age, but still a good horseman and a better doctor. He looked at Elsa for a moment before turning into the door of Nash's room. He said in his blunt fashion, 'Bette, I think Miss Nash needs as much nursing as her brother. See to her.'

Bette Mason laughed and turned to where Elsa stood by the closed door. Her pretty blondeness had always reminded Elsa of a china doll. But long ago she had found that that was only a surface picture that hid a wiry strength surprising in such a small woman and hid competence as well.

Bette stopped laughing quickly and went to Elsa to take her arm. 'I'm all right,' Elsa said. 'A little tired.'

Bette said shrewdly, 'They haven't found Carr yet.'

'Then they haven't found Pat, either.'

They looked at each other a moment and then both of them laughed lightly. Bette was allowed to take Elsa's arm now. She said, 'I'm sure Dad will want some coffee when he's done. And I'm sure you could use a cup.'

With the warmth of the kitchen enclosing her and the coffee on the table before her, Elsa felt some of the tension ease away. Bette's news had helped and now Bette's casual talk, her easy manner, was like a tonic. But neither of them could keep away from the subject and finally Elsa said, 'I promised Pat I'd talk to you.'

'Does he think I've lost my faith in him—because of this?'

'Many would,' Elsa answered. She met Bette's gaze. 'Many have.'

'And lost faith in Carr too,' Bette said abruptly. She rose and got the coffee pot and refilled their cups. When she was seated again, she went on, 'I nursed Carr in the hospital. He didn't have to fight Neil Griff. I went with Dad to the L-in-C when Carr was thrown from his horse. He didn't have to charge against a man holding a gun on him. Now he has defied the law.'

'Carr has his pride,' Elsa said.

Bette shook her head. 'But it was Pat who hit his pride. Yet he did those things—for Pat.'

Elsa said quietly, 'As Pat would have done them for Carr.'

'I want to think so,' Bette Mason answered.

Doctor Mason stamped into the kitchen, sniffing at the coffee smells. He accepted a cup and stood by the door sipping noisily. 'Your brother is awake,' he said to Elsa. 'And he's hungry. Did you bring that broth, Bette?'

'I even put it on the stove,' she said. 'I'll take it to him in a moment.'

'I can do that,' Elsa said quickly. 'You've been help enough already.'

Bette turned from the stove. 'If there's anything more . . .'

She left the rest unsaid. Her father finished his coffee at a gulp and set the cup down loudly. Then he looked at Elsa. 'Should anyone need a doctor soon,' he said, 'it would be better to take me to them than to bring them to me.' He picked up his bag and jammed his hat on his head. 'Come on, Bette, let her feed Nash. Give her something to do.'

'Thank you,' Elsa said. She remained at the table, not getting up to see them out, knowing that neither would take it as a breech of etiquette. At last she stood and poured some of the broth Bette had brought into a bowl and took it to her brother.

He lay propped on pillow, his face sallow, and no sign of fever left about him. He accepted the soup in silence, eating it slowly, shaking his head when she tried to help him. She stood and waited and, when he was done, took the bowl and started for the door.

He said in a surprisingly strong voice, 'Any news?'

She could not hide the gladness in her voice. 'No news.'

He looked at her steadily. 'Oh?'

She said almost desperately, 'Sim, Carr brought you in and tended you.'

'I have known killers who were kind to their wives and children,' he said shortly. 'It made them no less killers in the eyes of the law.' She could only stand and look at him. At last, he said, 'The doctor tells me I can be up in a day or two.'

She walked out then, leaving the words hanging in the air behind her, understanding, without thinking, the implication behind them.

CHAPTER SIX

The canyon Carr had chosen lay a short distance east of the Bowl. It was narrow-mouthed, little more than a hole, surrounded by sheer, bare walls and completely blocked except for a small entry screened by timber and buckbrush.

There was an overhang where a man could build a fire, and seepage from rocks where he could collect water. Otherwise, there was little to be said for the place, except that it was not even known to many who had lived a long time in this part of the country. Now Carr paced by the small fire, looking at the two men stretched out wearily on the ground before it. Ned Watts was out by the trail, standing guard.

Pat Tyler squinted up at the stars. 'I reckon it to be about ten o'clock. If they're coming with food, it's time they got here.'

'I'm glad we ate good when we did,' old Peak said. 'It's been thirty hours, about.'

'We had two grouse,' Tyler reminded him.

Two grouse for four hungry men was hardly enough, Carr thought, feeling the gnawing in his own stomach. And those they had trapped by hand because caution kept them from using their guns.

All during the day they had been able to hear men not too far from them. Once a group had ridden to the Bowl and then gone eastward along the trail that ran before the small canyon until it dwindled off against a cliff face. Carr, on watch then, had heard one man make the steep climb up to the old cabin still higher than they were. When the man returned, the group waiting for him rode off. Since then, there had been no sign of anyone.

Carr swung away from the fire. 'I'm riding down to the ranch to see if anything is wrong. Nash may have come and arrested them.'

'Shot as he is?' Tyler asked.

Carr said without humor, 'Nash would rise from a deathbed to prosecute his law, Pat.' He went to his horse and Tyler rose to join him.

78

'Stay here,' Carr ordered, 'It's easier for one man than two. There might be a watch on the place. That's the kind of thing Ogle would think of.'

'How long do we give you?' Tyler wanted to know.

Carr made a quick calculation. 'To dawn. If I'm not back by then, take the men over into Idaho or Canada—if you can make it.'

Tyler only grunted and walked away. Carr knew that if he wasn't back by dawn, they would come after him—not go the other way.

He followed the trail on the off side of the west ridge, guided by the moonlight but revealed by it as well. He rode cautiously, staying in shadow as much as he could and, when he reached the fir trees that marked the branching of the trail, drew into their shadow and stopped.

This trail, narrow and tenuous, broadened out here, one path going straight ahead to join the switchback road to town, the other, less used, angling across a corner of Ogle's land and leading to Carr's L-in-C. He chose the angled track, though it didn't go too far from Ogle's house. When he had followed it to the main trail leading to his own place, he stopped again.

He was not far from the L-in-C now and he had heard nothing, seen no one. Puzzled, he tied the horse and went forward carefully on foot. A low rise lay ahead and he dropped to

79

the ground as a man's figure appeared on it, silhouetted against the night.

The man stood in full view and Carr eased up the slope, testing each step before putting his foot down, careful of loose stones or twigs whose sound might give him away. He was within ten feet of the man when heavy footsteps came from ahead and another man joined the watcher. Carr huddled down, out of the moonlight, his eyes fixed on the pair now standing together at the top of the rise.

A voice said, 'Keep a sharp eye out, Larry. I figure if those T-Over men are going to try and contact Carr, this is about the time of night they'll try it.'

Carr recognized Ogle's voice and, as the other spoke, Larry Purvis'. 'Nothing stirring around here. I could stand a little relief myself.'

Ogle laughed, a short, bitter sound. 'There are five of us left. The townsmen decided that the responsibility was ours now that we're in the hills. And we'll be lucky if we can keep Larkin and Neely from riding for the saloon to warm themselves.'

Purvis said, 'They don't see it as their affair. No one took their cattle.' He sounded sick of the whole affair.

Carr thought, Five men. That didn't leave many to guard a place with as many potential exits as his. On the other hand, he had no way of knowing just where any one of the five would be at any given time.

'We'll find 'em,' Ogle said. 'They can't live off the country forever. And I don't think Carr is the kind to leave. We'll find 'em soon enough.'

'My place is going to hell,' Purvis grumbled. 'Let's make it soon.'

Ogle said something Carr didn't catch and then disappeared. Carr waited some time, listening to the fading of Ogle's heavy footsteps. Then, finally, Purvis grew restless and began to pace back and forth. One time he came so close to Carr that the make of the carbine he carried would have been recognizable in daylight. He passed on, stopped a few feet down the trail and turned back.

Carr thought, I could jump him. But he knew that meant raising a ruckus and he decided that the best plan was to do this as quietly as possible. When Purvis went over the brow of the hill, Carr took advantage of his going and slipped sideways through the brush, followed a meandering deer trail, and stunned finally not fifty yards from his own corral.

He could see a light in the house and that was all. Ogle, apparently, was keeping his men well back, hoping he had a trap set up.

Carr looked over the situation, picked his spots, and ran in short bursts from shadow to shadow until he was against the side of the bunkhouse. He stood there, getting his wind and listening. But there was no sound from beyond and he chanced a last sprint that carried him to the kitchen door and inside.

He eased the door shut behind him. 'Carr here,' he called.

'Ah.' It was Milo Carter and he came in with a lamp, holding it high, one hand on the gun at his waist.

Carr grinned as the hand dropped away. 'It's me, and I'm wolf hungry. So are the others.'

Milo set down his lamp and went to the larder. 'I'll whip up something you can carry.'

'Where are the boys?'

'Bettle is sleeping. Bill is out seeing if he can find a hole is Ogle's guard line. I'm keeping watch here. We been taking turn about.'

'Ogle has a guard set up around the place. He thinks I'll try to contact you, or vice versa.'

Milo Carter snickered. 'Getting bright, ain't he? We know about the guard; that's why we haven't been up to you. Ten men is a lot to sneak through.'

'There are only five left,' Carr said. He told Milo what he had overheard.

Milo only grunted and began slicing roast beef from a large, well-cooked chunk. When some was ready he handed it to Carr. 'They came in after we did last night and tried to push us around some. We pushed back by letting 'em see our carbines. They calmed down since, I reckon.'

'They haven't tried anything?'

82

Milo laughed and watched Carr lay the beef between two thick slices of bread and begin to eat. 'They been too busy chasing you to even bother with what's going on at T-Over.'

Carr wolfed the sandwich between gulps of stale coffee.

'Griff?'

'Griff,' Milo said. He was laughing no longer. 'Rick Bettle came in a little while ago and said Griff has begun his drive. He's pushing about fifty head over the Saddle right now.'

Carr finished his sandwich and began to shape a cigarette. 'What would Ogle say to that, I wonder?'

Milo snorted. 'Say? What is there to say? It's Government graze, ain't it? Griff's got his rights on there like the rest of you.'

Carr held a match against the hot stove and when it was flaming lighted his cigarette. 'If that's all Griff wanted, there'd been no need for all this, Milo. But we've always had an agreement about how much we'd graze in the valley. I don't think Griff will be satisfied with just his share.'

'T-Over's share,' Milo corrected him. 'You think you can make Ogle see that, go talk to him.' He turned away, filling a sack with food and cooking equipment.

Carr smoked in silence, feeling the strength run into him as the food he had eaten took hold. This move of Griff's was not surprising, although its suddenness was. Still, what better time was there for Griff to establish himself than during the confusion of this manhunt? More and more he began to see the neat way in which Griff had set up the situation and then taken advantage of every break to further his position.

Suddenly he smiled. An idea had occurred to him and the more he worked on it, the better he liked it. Griff wasn't the only man who could force a situation into the shape he wanted it.

He looked up at Milo. 'How many men has Griff got?'

Milo shrugged. 'Rick counted four on the drive. Griff wasn't one of 'em.' He handed Carr the heavy sack. 'There's enough here for a few days, I'd say. And be careful. Them pots in there might get loose and rattle.'

Carr thanked him and hoisted the sack to his shoulder. At the door, he stopped. 'If you get to town, Milo, and see Nash's sister—'

He stopped and Milo said, 'Yes?'

'Why, inquire after her brother's health,' Carr said dryly.

'Sure,' Milo said. He matched Carr's dryness. 'Any message for the Doc's girl from Pat?'

'We're all right,' Carr said. He opened the door. 'Keep an eye on the valley for us, Milo.'

When he was outside, he worked back the way he had come, making as good time as he had before, despite the weight of the sack on his back.

Larry Purvis was still guarding the rise when Carr reached it, and it took some time for Purvis to make up his mind to stroll on down the trail so that Carr could slip along after him. Carr stayed in shadow along the edge of the timber, moving slowly, waiting tensely for the moment when Purvis would turn and start back toward him.

He saw Purvis begin to turn not ten feet ahead of him and he started to draw off deeper into the brush. His horse was pretty close and he had his worst fears realized when the animal snuffled loudly, complaining of his loneliness.

Carr swore under his breath as Purvis turned back, peering into the bushes where the noise had come from. He seemed to locate it and he broke into a run, his carbine lifted Carr thought, He's edgy enough to shoot first and look afterward.

He broke into the open, hanging onto the sack as he ran. The sudden jouncing set the pans inside rattling against one another. Purvis stopped and turned, bewildered by the apparent attack from two directions. Carr wasn't five feet away now and he saw the carbine swing up, aimed for his middle.

He did the only thing there was to do. He threw the sack, heaving it over his shoulder in an arc that carried it onto Purvis. He staggered under the sudden weight, his gun going sideways, roaring its protest into the night. Carr followed the sack and, as Purvis threw it aside and straightened up, Carr hit him with all the force of his right arm. Purvis staggered again, this time crashing onto the trail on his back and lying still.

Carr didn't stop but grabbed the sack as he went past and raced for his horse. He untied the reins, pivoted into the saddle and rode as fast as the terrain would permit, fearing that Ogle and the others would be down on him after that shot.

He was back at the fir trees before he had the sack tied securely. He drew into their shadow and listened, but he could hear no sound over the breathing of his horse, and he turned up the trail and pushed the animal once more.

The fact that there was no organized pursuit did not surprise him. Ogle's interest, he knew, was in finding where they were hidden, not getting into a war with him at night. He would want to locate the hide-out quietly and then go for an army to besiege it.

Carr stopped now and then to rest the horse and to listen for sounds that would indicate that someone was following him at a safe distance. But he heard nothing until he reached the canyon and was challenged by Peak standing guard.

Carr called Peak to the fire with the other

men. 'There's no need to watch for a while,' he said. He laid the food out while he told them about Ogle's maneuver and Milo Carter's news.

Pat Tyler gnawed bread and beef and looked longingly at the coffee not yet boiling. 'Griff can only put so many head in there,' he said. 'We've got it grazed to the limit.'

'The limit of common sense,' Carr corrected. 'Anyway, who says Griff will leave our stock there?'

'It's Government graze,' Ned Watts said.

Peak scowled at him. 'The only law in these parts is laid up shot. Besides, I can't see Nash helping us.'

'That's what I mean,' Carr said. The coffee boiled and he poured it, handing the cups around. Then, squatting close to the small fire, he rolled a cigarette and lighted it. 'I have an idea that might work. It might get us caught, too,' he added.

Pat Tyler blew on his coffee. 'So might sitting here. Go on.'

Carr said, 'Griff pushes about fifty head into the valley tonight, according to Mile. What's to stop us from pushing them back out?'

Peak cackled and slapped a hand on his knee. 'Now what *is* to stop us?'

'Griff,' Ned Watts said.

'He won't waste manpower guarding it,' Carr said. 'Not when he's safe in the eyes of the law. No, Griff won't stop us—not the first

87

time anyway.'

'Ah,' Pat Tyler said when he saw what Carr was driving at. 'We don't run it back where it came from then?'

'No.'

Tyler grinned. 'What do we do when the Bowl is full?'

'By then,' Carr said, 'Griff will have done something.' He stood up. 'We gain nothing sitting here and waiting. We'll pull him out and hit him. And when he hits back, maybe he'll expose himself.' He looked soberly at the others. 'We're all tagged as rustlers. All right—then for a while, that's what we'll be.'

'By God,' Pat Tyler murmured. He gulped the last of his food, washed it down with scalding coffee and stood up. 'I'm ready.'

Peak and Ned Watts joined him. Carr smiled his pleasure and then detailed his suggestion. Ned Watts drew the job of staying on guard. The other three found their horses, took off the hobbles, and saddled up. Carr led the way out of the canyon and through the waning moonight to Rustler's Trail.

'We ride fast,' Carr said. 'If we don't make it by daylight, we don't do it.'

The Trail was a broad swath that a snowslide had cut long ago. It had since grown up here and there with bush and small trees but for the most part it was barren except for rock and rubble that the slide had left. They made fair time on the downslope and once on the level of the valley floor stepped up their pace.

Griff's cattle were still fairly well bunched off to one side and had drifted well away from the foot of the Saddle. Carr drew the men in some distance before they reached the herd and they eased up more slowly, watchful for guards. But there weren't any. The valley lay under the last of the moonlight, vast and empty but for the spots of darkness that marked bunches of beef scattered about.

With Griff's small herd still not at rest after their drive, it was fairly easy to get them moving. They were pushed at a faster pace than they liked, but with three men on them they stayed together and kept moving. At the foot of the Trail they had to slow but they were well up it when dawn cracked the rim of the dark over the eastern mountains.

Carr was stiff in the saddle, weary from the hard ride of earlier in the evening and the even harder push of the grind of keeping the cattle together and headed in the right direction. He could feel the remains of his bruises throbbing and the pain of his cracked ribs was a steady drain on him. When he stopped once and looked back to the first fingers of daylight creeping into the valley he knew that it had been worth the effort. For this once, at least, they had won. Unless one of Griff's men was standing guard at the top of the Saddle when daylight came and happened to be looking toward the Trail in the distance, no one could possibly see the herd before it was over the hump and out of sight.

Finally the small bunch was pushed into the Bowl—a small mountain meadow cupped in a ring of steep hills—a brush fence was hastily made across the opening, and the men returned wearily to their camp. By the time a meal was eaten, the sun could be seen eastward through the notch. Carr stretched to the fire.

'Our luck held,' he said. 'After this, we'll make it earlier.'

'After this?' Tyler questioned. 'Griff is no fool. He'll know what happened.'

'So I hope,' Carr said. 'I'd hate to think he'd let us go on taking his beef like this.'

They left before midnight the second time, leaving old Peak to stand guard. According to Ned Watts, the last man who had been lookout during the daylight, Griff's men had driven two small bunches from his big gather down on the Bunchgrass, up the wagon road and through the Saddle into the valley.

'I reckon around seventy-eighty head,' he said as they rode down the Trail.

'Keep an eye out tonight,' Carr warned 'There'll be no easy push like last night again.'

'My guess is, he'll have a crew laying for us,' Tyler said.

'Maybe,' Carr answered, 'but I think he'll wait for the law before he makes any kind of open attack.' He studied the moon-filled sky.

'Griff hasn't used much force yet, Pat. It's something he's saving for the time when he might really need it.'

Pat Tyler only grunted and they rode on in silence. When they hit the valley floor, they kept a steady pace, hugging the east wall where the shadows lay thickest, alert at each movement on the grass, stopping to investigate every unnatural sound before riding on.

Once, a lone heifer was spooked from her sleep and rose in front of them to go lowing off into the night. They waited some time before going on after that, but there was no sign that the disturbance had been loud enough to draw any guards Griff might have posted. They were almost to the point where the valley sides began their curve toward the Saddle when Carr drew rein, stopping the two men behind him.

'Someone ahead, to the right,' he whispered. They sat quietly, waiting, now and then moving enough to keep their horses from stirring too much. Finally a match flared ahead as a man on horseback lighted a cigarette. It was no one Carr had ever seen before.

'Listen!' he whispered. There was the sound of a horse being ridden toward the guard. It was coming fast but not too fast and it didn't make too much noise on the spongy grass floor of the valley.

'It's about time,' Carr said. 'No guns.'

They eased their horses forward in the darkness.

CHAPTER SEVEN

When Griff got the news that the fifty head he had had run into the valley had disappeared, he began to swear and then stopped, changing to laughter. He looked at Dutch, who had brought the story.

'So that's the way Lindon wants to play it.'

'By God,' Dutch said 'They must have run 'em up the Trail into the Bowl. Me and the boys'll get 'em back fast enough.'

Griff shook his head. 'Not yet,' he said quickly. 'This bears thinking about.' He paced the length of the parlor, smoking fitfully, stopping now and then to stare into the cold ashes in the fireplace as if to find an idea there.

'Go see that today's drive is moving, Dutch.'

'And let Lindon take that too?' Dutch demanded irately.

Griff looked at him, frowning. 'You think he'll try it in the daytime? Use your head. And do what I say!'

Dutch went out, shrugging, and Griff resumed his pacing. When Finley returned, he told him what had happened. Finley looked gloomy. 'I told you it wouldn't go easy, Neil. Even that fool Ogle will see soon enough what you're planning and try to stop you.'

'He won't see until I'm ready,' Griff said.

He smiled in faint contempt at Finley. 'Hasn't the owner of the T-Over a right to put his share of beef into the valley?'

'His share, yes. But when Leaning-G beef covers the valley you can't claim the whole thing is your share.'

'By then,' Griff said, 'I won't care. Dutch tells me the big herd is almost to the flats. By the time it arrives, we'll have the smaller bunch into the valley and then make the big push. What can Ogle say when it's all in? What can Ogle do against us?'

'Not Ogle, maybe,' Finley grumbled, 'but there's Lindon.'

'I'm going to let Lindon outsmart himself,' Griff murmured. 'Starting tonight.'

At supper, he gave Dutch his orders. 'You send two men—no more tonight—to ride that herd. How many did you drive in?'

'About eighty,' Dutch said. He was still frowning. 'You let me handle it, Boss, and—'

'I said two men,' Griff told him. 'How many has Lindon got? Four at the most, counting himself.'

Finley said, 'Those three T-Over men on Lindon's place?'

Griff laughed. 'Ogle has them bottled up for us.' He glanced at Dutch. 'And tomorrow, drive the rest of the stuff in. How many left?'

'Sixty or so, but the big bunch will be in late tomorrow.'

'Leave them for the next day,' Griff said.

'Give them a rest.' He leaned back with a cigar, looking satisfied with himself.

Dutch grumbled, but he passed on the order and chose a pair Griff had sent for from among those who were coming with the big bunch from Spokane Falls.

'You, Lefty,' he said, nodding to a tall, dish-faced man. 'And Mitch. Get some sleep—Boss wants you to ride nightherd on that drive we made today.'

Mitch, a squat, bull-built man, swore. 'Nightherd in that valley?'

'Nightherd in that valley,' Dutch said again. 'And keep your eyes peeled or you'll lose 'em.' He gave them a brief picture of Carr Lindon and Pat Tyler. Before he left, he said, 'Go down about ten.'

The moon was high, though on the wane now, as the two men dropped into the valley. The herd had worked itself into one bunch and was drifting northward, cropping the fine, rich grass, not making much of a fuss. Mitch put Lefty east of the Saddle and not far from it and then rode northwestward near where the tail of the herd was. Soon it had settled down, bedding for the night, and only the restless sounds of a few still-moving animals were heard. Mitch yawned and left his saddle for the more comfortable grass.

He thought he could feel the faint shaking of the ground that a group of riders would make and came alert, climbing on his horse again and trying to break apart the shadows formed on the moonlit graze. But there was nothing and soon he got down and walked around to keep himself awake.

He was glancing back toward the Saddle, thinking of the bunkhouse and the bed in it, when he saw the light. It was a mere flicker, brief and sharp and then gone. He swore. 'That fool Lefty.'

He caught his horse, mounted, and rode for the other man, taking care not to go too fast, to keep the pound of the horse's hoofs as soft as possible. If this Lindon and his crew had come, he thought, that match was a signal for trouble.

He was almost to where he had left Lefty when he heard the sound. It was faint, a grunting, then a thud as though someone had hit the ground with his body.

He reined in, waiting. The shadows were deep here and Mitch could feel the cold of the night air along the base of his neck. Finally, he drew his gun and eased the horse forward. 'Lefty? Lefty?'

'Yeh?'

It was just a voice coming from the darkness to his left. Mitch reined that way, and the voice came from where he had just been. 'Yeh?'

He swung his horse frantically, his gun up, his eyes straining to pierce the dark. He felt more than heard the other horse come along his off side, and before he could turn there was

95

the sound of wind in his ears and then a great roaring as a gun butt drove down against the side of his head. He pitched off his horse, thudding as he landed, and lay still.

* * *

'I don't like it,' Carr said. 'It's too easy.'

Tyler shrugged and reached for the coffee pot. It was nearing the time to ride to the valley again, and all of them were getting restless.

'What do you expect, with Ogle still keeping watch on the L-in-C, the sheriff shot, and from what you heard Ogle say, the town no longer interested.'

'I'm thinking about Griff as much as any of them,' Carr said. 'How long will he let us push him around before he hits back?' He frowned into the darkness that lay just beyond the edge of the narrow circle of firelight. The first time it had been easy because Griff had not expected an attack. But he could not fathom the man's reason for putting only two guards out last night, and two men obviously untrained to this sort of thing, at that.

Carr thought of the ridiculous ease with which they had captured the first man and then maneuvered the second into position. It didn't fit the pattern he had built for Griff's actions.

'He's liable to have a full crew down there

tonight,' Carr said

Pat Tyler squinted at the stars and rose. 'We'll soon find out,' he said.

All four rode tonight, none of them seeing any reason to guard what little there was left of their stock of food. They cached it well under the overhang, doused the fire, and left. The moos was sliding toward third quarter now, and there was just light enough for them to pick their way along the trail. Carr halted at the point where Rustler's Trail broke into the one they were on and sat motionless a moment, staring down toward the valley. Then he turned to Peak on his right.

'You say about sixty head came in today?'

'About. All in one drive,' the old man answered. He sounded impatient.

Carr said thoughtfully, 'If two of us could come in by way of the Saddle and the other two go in like we have before, we can keep from being squeezed.'

Tyler thought it over. He said, 'It means running through Ogle, too.'

'I doubt if he has more than Purvis and Jerry Dyke left to him,' Carr answered. 'Standing long watches for someone else is nothing town drinkers like to do.'

Tyler said roughly, 'What difference does it make? I'll ride with you.'

Carr directed Peak and Ned Watts to follow the same pattern they had used the night before, then swung westward along a narrow path that led through a small cut onto a barren flat and joined the trail that went along the off side of the west flats. It was the way he had gone to L-in-C the other night but now he rode more carefully, thinking that Ogle might have a man posted here somewhere.

At the junction, by the clump of firs, they turned eastward, riding even more slowly now. Near the rise where he had seen Larry Purvis, Carr signaled a halt. 'We walk from here,' he said in a low voice.

They went on foot, leading their horses, stopping every few steps to listen. But there was no sound beyond those of the forest itself. A light breeze soughed through the tops of the firs, and occasionally a small night animal scurried in the underbrush. That was all.

They reached the edge of the L-in-C yard and stopped again, looking down at the light glowing from the kitchen window.

'Late for someone to be up,' Carr said.

'Milo, most likely,' Tyler responded. 'He spends half the night prowling the cupboard and drinking coffee and then complains he can't sleep.'

Carr studied the light, thinking of the lack of noise, of opposition, and he disliked it. Still he had a decision to make and not too much time to make it in. He said, 'We need information. Let's go.'

They mounted now and rode openly toward the kitchen door. The sound of their coming was clear on the night air yet the door did not open. Pat Tyler said softly, 'That isn't like Milo, Carr. He'd be out to see who was coming. I say break and run.'

'And if someone has Milo and the boys held in there?' Carr asked.

'Ah,' Pat Tyler said. 'I hadn't thought of that.' He leaned forward in the saddle and raked his spurs lightly into his horse's flanks. Carr opened his mouth to stop him and saw that it was too late. Tyler would be at the rear door before he could get the sound out. He threw a heel into his horse.

'Move, fellow,' he said.

Tyler left the saddle before his horse stopped, lit running, and plowed on to the door. He had it open and was framed in the light when Carr reined up.

From behind them, by the bunkhouse, a voice said, 'That's far enough, both of you.'

Pat Tyler turned, his hand going for his gun, and a carbine went off behind Carr, the bullet slapping wood just above Tyler's head. Tyler stood where he was, not moving, his face bitter. Carr dropped to the ground and stood in the shadow by his horse, waiting.

'I messed it up again,' Tyler said angrily. 'I—'

Carr lifted his voice. 'All right. All right. You've had your fun.'

He heard someone coming from the bunkhouse. Mort Ogle appeared behind Tyler in the kitchen doorway, a hand gun in his heavy fist.

'No fun,' he said. 'No fun at all.'

Two of them, Carr thought. There would be at least three. Ogle seldom went anywhere without Purvis or Jerry Dyke. Now Purvis came into the light and Carr said, 'Where's Jerry?'

'At the corner,' Ogle said. There was satisfaction in his voice. 'You're boxed, Carr.'

Still Carr did not move. 'What did you do with the T-Over men?'

'They aren't hurt,' Ogle said.

Carr said slowly, 'We've been running Griff's beef out of the valley, Mort.'

'So I know. He was in town today and swore a warrant out for all of you—for rustling and attacking his men.'

So that was it, Carr thought. That was why only two guards had been put on last night. He said, 'What will you do when Griff's beef covers the valley, Mort?'

'Griff will take no more than his share,' Ogle said heavily. 'He told me so.'

This was no use, Carr saw. Words were no way to get around Ogle. Not now. He said easily, 'Might as well go in where it's comfortable.'

'You're going to town,' Ogle said. 'The jailhouse is comfortable enough.' He prodded Tyler with his gun.

Tyler stepped forward slowly, hesitantly.

Another prod and he moved on toward his horse, Ogle following. As if it had been a signal, Jerry Dyke came around the corner of the house, a carbine cradled in his arm. Purvis moved in from his position, his gun ready.

'Get ropes and our horses,' Ogle said to Purvis. He turned toward the barn.

Carr took a deep breath, lifted his hand and slapped his horse on the rump with all the strength he could muster. 'Go, fellow!'

The horse let out a snort of surprise, flicked out its heels, and dashed forward. Purvis stopped and turned, trying to swing his gun around. Carr yelled, 'Now, Pat!' and drew, firing as he did so, sending a bullet screeching over Jerry Dyke's head.

Pat Tyler swung about fluidly as if he had been waiting for this. His left arm chopped at Ogle's gun, driving it downward, and his right made a short arc, catching Ogle in the throat, sending him backward, gasping for air. Tyler fell as he struck, diving on top of Ogle. He rolled off and came to his knees, Ogle's gun in his hand.

Purvis and Dyke stood stupidly, men unaccustomed to action, confused by the commotion. Carr said, 'Drop those guns.'

Purvis looked toward him, the light from the kitchen doorway showing the twisted frustration on his long face. Carr said, 'I might not shoot to miss this time, Larry. A man gets tired of being pushed around.'

The gun dropped. Jerry Dyke tossed his aside angrily. 'By God, Carr, you can't go on forever. We'll get you sooner or later and then—'

'And then,' Carr said, 'it won't matter one way or the other, Jerry. Then Griff will have it all. All right, inside—and take Mort with you.'

The two men picked Ogle up and half-carried him, half-dragged him inside to the parlor as Carr had directed. Leaving Tyler to watch, he holstered his gun and worked over Ogle, bringing his breath back. When the man stopped choking, Carr went to the cupboard and brought the whiskey bottle. Ogle took a brief drink and then sat breathing heavily, staring down at his hands.

Carr went through the small house and returned. 'Where are they?' he demanded. His voice was flat and cold.

'Not hurt, I told you,' Ogle said. 'They're in the barn with our horses.'

Carr found them, well tied but not too uncomfortable, lying in a row in the hay. When his gag was removed, Milo Carter started to swear, not stopping until he had no more breath left.

'How did it happen?' Carr said mildly.

'Purvis came slipping up like it was you, Carr. In the dark, we thought it was,' Rick Bettle said. He rubbed his wrists where the ropes had held him. 'He came in and got the drop and the rest was easy.'

'From their talk,' Milo said when he had his breath back, 'they saw you coming down the trail and decided to get you here as being the easiest way.'

'Almost,' Carr said. He was shaking a little, thinking how foolish they had almost been. 'Let's go in.'

When they reached the parlor, Tyler had all three men lined up on the sofa. 'What do we do with them?' he demanded. The anger at himself was still in him, reddening his face, making him truculent.

'Why,' Carr said, 'we keep them out of trouble.' His humor bit at the three. 'They don't use brains enough to keep out of it for themselves.' He turned to Milo Carter. 'Got some rope handy?'

Milo brought it and, under Carr's direction, the T-Over men had the satisfaction of tying up the men who had given them the same treatment a short while before. After that, their horses were brought and they were roped into the saddles.

Carr said, 'Mort, this is my property. I could file a complaint against you for breaking and entering. The next time you choose to come here, do so in daylight with your hands up.' His voice roughened. 'Any one of you caught on my land after this can expect to get shot.'

Mort Ogle did not answer. He sat tightly roped into the saddle, his head hanging, his heavy body slumped. Carr said to Milo Carter,

'Can you take them near Ogle's place and then turn their horses loose? They'll drift up to where Mort's wife can find them.'

'Pleasure,' Milo Carter said, and turned to get a horse.

Carr and Tyler loaded two sacks with food, tied them to their saddles, and mounted their horses. Carr said to the two remaining T-Over men, 'If you see any one of them on L-in-C land, use your own judgment.'

Old Bill Marcus spat. 'I'll shoot once high. Their hands don't go up, I'll lower my sights.'

'And when you see the sheriff,' Carr said, 'tell him about it. You're the law on this property now.' He rode off into the darkness, Tyler a half pace behind.

They moved in silence, knowing that there was more danger ahead than that which they left behind them. Here they were nearing Neil Griff's men, and they were not the kind to be taken in by the simple trick Carr had used a half hour before.

But there was no one patrolling the Saddle when they looked down upon it. There was no one within sight or sound as they eased their horses down the steep slope to the Saddle and then rode softly to the valley floor. The valley lay stretched in the last of the moonlight, silent except for the stirrings of sleeping cattle.

'I don't like it,' Carr said. 'Where are Peak and Ned? Where—'

'Listen,' Tyler said sharply.

104

Carr quieted his breathing and listened to the distant windborne sounds. Slowly he sorted them out—the restless cattle, the night cry of coyote, the wind itself brushing the tree tops, and then the sound of horses' hoofs on rock, the faintest of tinkling sounds. And above it the heavy rumble such as a herd of cattle being pushed at a good clip will make on hard ground.

'Up the Trail,' he said.

They headed northward, pushing their horses now, paying no attention to the noise they made. At the foot of the Trail they slowed, having to pick their way along the rocky path. And halfway up it, they stopped sharply, brought up by the crackle of old Peak's voice.

'Who's riding?'

Carr identified them quickly, not liking the brittle excitement in the old man's voice. Peak said, 'You took long enough. Another hour and we'd had these in the Bowl by ourselves.'

'What about Griff's guards?' Carr demanded.

'Weren't none. Wasn't nobody,' Peak said.

They rode on, pushing the beef ahead of them. Carr was silent, turning this over in his mind. But he could find no answer, no reason for Griff acting so. He only knew that it was wrong—it didn't have the right ring to it.

CHAPTER EIGHT

A touch on his shoulder awakened Carr in midmorning. He sat up, blinking against a shaft of sunlight that struck across his eyes. Pat Tyler stood at the edge of the overhang.

'They're coming,' he said.

Carr was on his feet, reaching for his gun belt hung on a peg he had driven into the rock near by. 'Griff?'

'Griff's men,' Tyler said. 'Dutch and Perly—the ones who were with Griff the night I was caught—and three more. They're coming up the Trail.'

'Ah,' Carr murmured, 'looking for beef, I suppose?'

He washed his face quickly, letting the chill of the water bring him fully awake. The coffee pot was on the fire and he poured a cup, hot and thick, and gulped at it while he drew on his boots and checked his gun.

Tyler said, 'What now? Do we let them take the cattle back?'

'Not yet,' Carr said. He saw that old Peak was bringing his horse and he walked to meet them. 'Let's see how they'll take a little more pushing around.' He glanced about. 'Where's Ned?'

'Up by the Bowl.'

When Peak reached him, Carr said, 'We'll

get in the rocks around the mouth of the Bowl. Let them get into six-gun range.' He looked at Tyler. 'And shoot to miss unless they get too rough, Pat. Remember, as far as the law is concerned, Griff has a right to those cattle.'

'I'll remember,' Tyler said, sounding as though he would prefer to have it otherwise.

They rode the short distance quickly, pulling their horses into timber, and moving onto the rocks on foot. Carr saw Ned Watts at a point above him peering down the Trail and now and then ducking his face back. His voice floated down.

'Five minutes away, maybe,' he said

Carr chose a spot where he had a good view of the top of the Trail, where it broke over the last rise, and he settled down to wait. It was a clear day with a slight breeze blowing into his face and he saw no danger in smoking a cigarette. He was grinding it out when he heard the distant clink of horseshoes on rock, the creak of saddle leather, and even the soft snort of a laboring horse.

'Ready.' His voice was low but loud enough for Tyler to his right and Peak to the left and below to hear him.

A five-man crew came into sight. One of them, Carr saw, was the dish-faced man who had been foolish enough to light a cigarette while on guard two nights before. He knew none of the others by sight, though he found it easy enough to identify the solid blond man as

Perly. The squat, dark one beside Perly would be Dutch, Carr thought.

They came on steadily, riding openly now, with an arrogant disregard for what might be against them, reminding Carr in that of Neil Griff. He let them get within easy range and then lifted his voice.

'That's far enough, friend.'

Dutch reined in and the others followed suit. He sat squinting into the sun in an effort to locate the voice. Carr spoke again. 'Go back the way you came,' he said.

Dutch's dark face twisted into a grin. 'Lindon? We got some cattle up here we're taking back with us.'

Carr's voice flattened out, 'I said ride back.' He lifted his gun, laid it on the rock, took careful aim and fired, the bullet singing from a rock just in front of Dutch's horse.

'One shot over their heads,' he ordered.

Dutch's mount reared with the closeness of the bullet, then reared again as three guns fired almost as one. Swearing, Dutch sawed the reins savagely. Perly's horse went sideways and both animals collided. The three men just behind them held their horses with tight grips and then the two in front calmed down. No one moved.

'You figure that'll get you anywhere?' Dutch demanded. His crooked grin came again. 'Griff wants his cattle back and he'll get 'em, one way or another.'

'He's welcome to them,' Carr said. 'Let him come and prove they're his stock.'

'They all got burned with the same iron,' Dutch said. 'Leaning-G.'

'That brand means nothing to me,' Carr said. 'I never heard of it.' His voice was faintly mocking, challenging.

For a moment Dutch was still and then he said savagely, 'You will, Lindon, you will.'

'You had our warning,' Carr said. 'Now ride back to Griff.'

Dutch was grinning again, as if completely sure of himself. 'I came for some cattle, Lindon.'

Carr leveled his gun again and fired, sending a second bullet at the feet of Dutch's horse. But this time Dutch was prepared and the animal only jerked against the tight rein curbing him.

'Next time I won't miss,' Carr said flatly. 'Ride!'

Dutch looked at his men, still displaying his amusement. 'Shall we ride, boys? Sheriff'll be interested in this, likely.' Turning his horse, he started slowly back down the Trail. One by one, the men fell in behind him.

Carr stayed where he was, watching them grow smaller as they worked their way along the rubble-strewn ground toward the valley floor. Finally he crawled from the rocks and went to his horse. The others joined him, none of them speaking; at the moment there seemed nothing to say.

'I'll take watch until dinnertime,' Carr said.

He rode restlessly back and forth on the narrow trail, patrolling from the point where the Bowl began to the twin larch trees that marked the turn-off to the entrance of their hideaway. Now and then, he left his horse and climbed up the rocks to look down Rustler's Trail. But if Griff was sending anyone, he was not coming by that route.

At dinnertime, old Peak relieved Carr. He said, 'Watch from the rocks now and then in case they send another delegation.'

'Ought to have shot that one up,' Peak grumbled. 'That's the only argument Griff'll ever understand.'

Carr said dryly, 'And one he has men enough to win, too.' He rode back to the camp.

In midafternoon Pat Tyler relieved the old man. He had only been gone a few minutes when Carr heard the strong beat of a horse being ridden rapidly, and he moved back into the overhang, reaching for his carbine.

It was Tyler returning. He swung his horse almost to where Carr stood, his face twisted with anger. 'Griff outsmarted us,' he said.

'Another crew coming?'

'Worse,' Tyler said. He sounded almost as if he were crying, the anger was shaking him so.

Carr and Ned Watts got their horses and followed Tyler to the mouth of the Bowl. Old Peak was perched high on the rocks, staring into the valley below. When they reached him, he was swearing softly and steadily, and his hand shook as he pointed southward.

'Look at that.'

Carr looked. From this vantage point, he could see the Trail, first crossing the valley and then to where the Saddle made a sharp indentation in the southern rimrock. It was a long look but things stood out sharply on a clear day such as this. From where they stood, it appeared that a great brown and white worm was undulating over the Saddle and down to the green valley floor. Once there, it spread in an ever-widening fan. There seemed no end to it. The Saddle was choked solid and the far end of the valley floor was half covered—with cattle.

'There, east!' Ned Watts said.

Carr saw what he meant. Specks that resolved themselves into men on horseback were working, cutting their horses back and forth, driving small bunches of cattle toward the narrow neck of land at the northeast end of the valley. Carr did not need to be any closer to realize what was happening.

'Griff is corralling our stock and bringing his own in,' he said. And he understood the anger that had its grip on Pat Tyler.

'Lots of his stuff,' Ned Watts said in his brief fashion.

Carr studied the wave of brown and white. 'Lots of it,' he agreed bleakly.

Tyler tried to roll a cigarette and gave it up as he spilled the tobacco onto the rocks before him. 'He must have as much in there as the five of us own put together,' he said. His voice burst out suddenly. 'By God, I should have shot him when I had the chance.'

'And be charged with murder along with everything else,' Carr said quietly. 'That's not the way to settle this, Pat.'

Tyler turned on him savagely. 'What is, then? What good did our running his couple of hundred head up to the Bowl do?'

'Got the law on us worse,' old Peak suggested.

'We've forced a showdown,' Carr pointed out. 'We made him play his hand—and maybe before he was ready.'

'Ah!' Tyler cried. 'He let us take those to keep us busy while he readied these.'

'Maybe,' Carr agreed. 'But we've started hitting him. Let's keep on.'

'Bowl ain't big enough,' Ned Watts said.

'That job's done,' Carr said. 'Now it's time for—' he stopped. Time for what? With three men here and three bottled up at the L-in-C, what could he do? What were six men against the dozen or more trained fighters Griff would have? Carr realized that even though they had forced Griff's hand, the man had, in the long run, turned the trick back against them.

He could see now why Griff had had no men guarding the herd last night. The two hundred head were of no great moment to him, since he well knew they could be taken nowhere but to the Bowl. And, Carr thought, with helpless anger, Griff would be able to get them back any time he really set his mind to it. He not only had his own men—and it would take a good dozen or better to do the work that was being done down there now—but he had worked it so that Ogle pressed Carr from one side and the law from the other.

'Ogle!' Carr said. He turned to Tyler. 'What would Mort say to this?'

'What difference does that make?' Tyler demanded.

Carr said quickly, 'We haven't a chance, Pat, unless we get enough men to match Griff—or come close to it. All right, there are seven of us, counting your men. But if we could get Ogle to stop being blind, we'd have a few more. Ten, at least. Maybe a dozen.'

'One's all I need,' Tyler said. 'One man, one bullet.'

Carr put a hand out, gripping Tyler's shoulder. 'You've bulled your way too often lately, Pat. And where did it get you?'

Tyler started to shrug the hand away and then stopped. He looked at Carr and the two men standing silently beside him and then down into the valley. 'By God,' he whispered. 'By God!' As if he had just realized the strength of Carr's friendship.

'You mean, where did it get *you*?'

'Forget that,' Carr said. 'If it hadn't been this way, Griff would have tried it another.'

Tyler forced a grin to his lips. 'All right, fellow. I'll cool down.'

Carr relaxed a little, letting relief run through him. He had felt hamstrung, unable to do anything with Tyler on a short fuse as he had been. He said now, 'I'm going to find Ogle, and make one more try.'

He clambered down the rocks to his horse and lifted himself into the saddle. 'Keep your eyes open. After this morning, Griff might try to finish them off in a hurry. He's pressing now: You can see it from what's down in the valley. And he's waited too long now to come after us, it seems to me.'

'I know Griff, Carr,' Tyler said. 'He'll figure you to ride for Ogle about this. Or the law.'

'So he might,' Carr agreed. He lifted a hand and rode off, following the same trail that he had the other night. Once on level ground he pushed his horse.

As he rode, he turned over in his mind the way Griff had worked this. The coming of Dutch he saw as a ruse to keep them occupied while Griff got his big drive started. And, at the same time, by driving the men away, Carr was tying one more legal knot around his and his men's necks.

Tyler's warning came to his mind and he glanced about him, wondering if Griff had men waiting for him to do just this—break for

Ogle and ride into a trap. Or maybe Griff would do it the simpler way and hope he would ride for the law—and let Nash arrest him. But as far as Carr could see, there would be no complaint for him to make. Not to a man like Sim Nash. Griff had broken no law openly yet. No written law, such as Nash would recognize, Carr added bitterly to himself.

With an effort he shook off the gloom that clamped itself over him. The clump of firs that marked the junction was visible now. He was not far from making contact with Ogle. And if he could get him to understand, then maybe Griff wouldn't have things all his own way.

He was within three hundred yards of the firs when a horse and rider broke into sight around them. Carr reined in, his hand dropping to his gun butt.

Then as the rider swept toward him, he saw that it was Elsa Nash and he let his hand fall from the gun. A moment later another horse came from behind the trees. It was Mort Ogle and he rode a horse that closed the gap between himself and Elsa rapidly.

Carr kicked his heels into his horse's flanks, but before he could get within good hand-gun range, Ogle was alongside Elsa, reaching to stop her horse.

Elsa pitched in the saddle and when she was straight again, she had her carbine from its boot. She swung it by the barrel and jabbed, driving the butt deliberately at Ogle's face.

Ogle's hands went up and he clawed air; then he pitched out of the saddle and lay spread-eagled on the ground.

Elsa came on, the carbine still in one hand. Her head came up as she saw Carr bearing down on her. She shouted something he couldn't understand and pointed to his left, sawing at the reins to halt her galloping horse.

He turned in the saddle and had a glimpse of the man not far above on the west ridge. His eye caught the glint of sunlight on metal and he tried to make his mount weave, but he moved too late. The crack of the gun was on the chill air. He felt the searing bite of the bullet, saw the ground rise up to meet him. Tyler's warning came to his mind and he realized that he had ridden into Griff's trap. Then there was the crashing sensation of all breath being driven from his body and he remembered no more.

CHAPTER NINE

Elsa Nash watched in silence as her brother walked from one end of the small parlor to the other and then back again. He had been doing this periodically since yesterday and the steady sound of his footfalls was beginning to rub her nerves.

She had dreaded the moment when he

would be able to get out of bed, but she had nursed him carefully, doing everything possible to get him on his feet quickly. It was not in her nature to be deceitful and, though the pity she had first felt when he had been shot had disappeared, she could not find it in herself to neglect him.

Since dinnertime today she had watched his strength grow. She knew now that soon he would be ready to ride and hunt for Carr.

A rider came up outside and stopped. Both Nash and Elsa were silent, waiting. The footfalls on the veranda were heavy, though the knock that came was quick and light. Nash himself crossed the room and drew the door open.

It was Neil Griff and when he saw Nash he smiled with pleasure. 'I was hoping to see you about, Sheriff. You're looking stronger than at my last visit.'

'Strong enough,' Nash replied shortly. He stepped aside to let Griff in. 'You have business?'

Griff removed his hat and bowed formally to Elsa. 'Miss Nash,' he murmured. He turned to the sheriff. 'Business,' he said. 'Lindon and his crew took another herd of my stuff last night. This morning I sent some men up to the Bowl to look for the cattle and they were driven off.' He paused and added, 'With guns.'

Nash sat down, his face expressionless, although Elsa knew that there was still a good deal of pain racking him. She was mending clothes and she kept her eyes on her work, her needle moving steadily while Griff talked.

'Did your men fight back?' Nash asked.

Griff laughed sharply. 'Fight back—with four guns on them? They didn't even draw.'

'And you want my help to get your cattle back?'

'You're the law,' Griff said smoothly. 'I have a right to protect my property—but that's public land up there.'

'The cattle are still yours,' Nash said dryly. He rose and took another turn about the room. He was testing his strength, Elsa knew.

'I'll ride,' he said decisively.

'If you need my help or any men . . .' Griff left his words hanging in the air, bowed again to Elsa, and left almost abruptly.

Nash waited until he had ridden away and then went to his room. He reappeared shortly, dressed for the trail, buckling his gun belt around his waist.

Now as Elsa looked at him, she made no effort to conceal the hostility in her eyes. 'What would you have done in Carr's place?' she demanded.

'I wouldn't have gotten into his place to begin with,' he answered.

'Do you ever give a man a chance?'

'Not a lawbreaker,' he said coldly.

'Who made him one but you!' she cried. 'Is there no difference to the law between a man who is a deliberate criminal and one who risks his life to do what he thinks right? Does the fact that he took a chance on his freedom to tend you mean nothing?'

He was testing his gun. 'Loving the man has blinded you, Elsa. He's as guilty as Tyler. And Tyler is a confessed rustler.'

She said swiftly, 'You believe Tyler when he talks about himself. You don't believe him when he warns you about Griff. What kind of law is that?'

'My kind. I have no proof against Neil Griff.'

'And you want none.'

'I have my eye on him,' Nash said. 'But there is no evidence that he has done anything illegal. When there is—if there is—I can act.' He picked up his hat. 'There's no argument, Elsa. The law is the law. It can work only one way—it touches everything and everyone equally.'

She blocked his way as he started from the house. 'Then arrest me. I unlocked the cell and turned Pat Tyler loose.'

As weak as he was, he still had the strength to bring pain when he grasped her shoulders. His expression was without any sign of compassion. 'If that was true,' he said, 'if I believed that, you'd be in a cell fast enough.'

She regarded him in surprise. He meant what he said. He saw the law through one narrow hole. Almost too late, Elsa realized

119

that she might taunt him too far. And she would be of no use in a cell—of no use to Carr.

She jerked free of him and stood rubbing her shoulders.

He said 'Is that true?'

She remembered something he had said, and it gave her the courage to laugh at him. 'The law requires proof, Sim. Do you have any?'

He stared at her in his still, frightening way. Then he turned and stalked out, moving carefully as a hurt man will, but walking erect, hiding his pain even from himself.

She watched him go and for the first time in her life she discovered that she was truly frightened of this cold, implacable men who was so consumed by his passion for the law— his kind of law. She whispered to herself, 'Law but not justice.' And she realized that justice did not exist in the mind of Sim Nash. The word held no meaning for him.

For a moment weakness caught her and she found that she was trembling. She sat, drawing deep breaths, wondering what there was she could do—she must do. For now that her brother was riding again, she knew he would not stop until he was dead or Carr and Tyler were in jail. And if it came to a showdown fight, what then?

She pushed the sewing away from her lap and rose. She had to see Carr, to warn him that her brother was riding.

She dressed in the jeans and flannel shirt she wore when she rode. She had a .38 with holster and belt which her brother had given her some years before and now she buckled them about her waist in addition, she got a carbine and this she put in the saddle boot when she had her horse ready.

She rode to the foot of the switchback and she could see her brother far above, moving slowly up the steep trail, riding carefully to husband his strength. She sat quietly a moment to consider this. If she followed him, she might be seen and even if she were not, there was no way to go around him and reach - the high country first. She thought of the Saddle and wondered if there might not be some way from there she might go.

She remembered Milo Carter coming in this morning to inform Nash that he was going to protect Carr s property with a gun if need be. She had felt anger at what he described as an invasion by Ogle. Now she thought, Pat's men will be at Carr's. Surely one of them could tell her how to get through to the high country, or could take the message himself.

When she reached the junction, she encountered a slowly moving but apparently endless mass of cattle. She reined back and watched as they poured off the bunchgrass flat, filled the road with their bulk and dust and lowing, and flowed up the gentle slope and out of sight. The brand on their flanks meant nothing to her.

A rider appeared out of the dust on the flank, tipped his hat to her, and started on. She said quickly, 'What herd is this?'

'Griff's, ma'am. Ain't there a mess of 'em, though?' He rode away, back into the dust.

Still not understanding fully the meaning of this, Elsa followed the man, working her way along the flanks of the moving herd, slowed now and then when she had to leave the road, and finally reached the top. Here the road surface was wider and she could make better time. At the junction to Carr's L-in-C, she hesitated and then went straight ahead toward the Saddle.

She drew rein there, on a slope off the road, and looked out across the valley, gazing down on the broad green carpet of grass. She had been here innumerable times and each time she had noted with pleasure the wise way in which the ranchers kept the beef down to avoid overgrazing. But today, as far as the valley stretched, there were thick patches of bunched brown and white. There must be four times the usual number already, she thought, and that endless herd still pouring up from the flats.

While she watched, a small bunch was cut out of the fairsized herd that grazed eastward, at a distance from the new stuff coming in. Her eyes followed the movements of the two men doing the cutting, and she saw that the cattle were being driven into enclosures made by fencing off the narrow neck at the northeast end of the valley. The reason for this puzzled her until she noticed that the cattle being fenced in were different stock from that coming dower over the Saddle.

When understanding came to her, she could only sit and stare. The audacity of Griff's actions stunned her. Then she moved, reining her horse about, thinking that this was some thing she must show to Sim.

She had barely started her horse when a rider came working his way through the stream of cattle flowing over the Saddle. She stopped, seeing that it was Neil Griff. He drew rein and doffed his white hat.

'Enjoying a ride, Miss Nash?'

There was something a bit too smooth in his voice, a faint mockery that stirred a warning within her. But when she answered, her voice was casual enough.

'I was just wondering at the change below, Mr. Griff.'

'A change of brand, that's all,' he said smoothly. He rode closer to her. 'Those cattle behind the fence are coming out; the new herd stays.' His eyes moved across her face.

But there was nothing there to see. Elsa had a strong grip on herself now and she met his gaze easily. 'I'm afraid I'm on private land,' she murmured. 'Am I intruding?'

'You're very welcome,' he said, and even his

gallantry seemed to her to be mocking.

'Are the ranchers as welcome?' she countered.

His eyes glinted with amusement and she knew she had been clumsy. 'Any man can ride my land, Miss Nash.'

'But not drive cattle across it?'

He did not take the bait. He said simply, 'There is only so much grass. I am unfortunately cursed with a great number of cattle. I brought them here because I heard there was unlimited range. It seems that such is not the case.' He shrugged. 'But they are here, and they must have something to eat.'

She sat silently. He tipped his hat, swung about, and worked his way down into the valley. She followed his progress until he reached the floor and then she lifted her eyes, looking beyond to the Trail flowing upward to the high country.

She saw her brother again. He had managed to work down from the west ridge to the Trail near its lower end. Her impulse to ride to him, to tell him what Griff was doing, faded under the realization that it would be wasted effort. For he could see this as well as she; he did not need to be told. And, she thought, Griff was making no attempt to hide what he did. He would be too clever a man to expose himself by being openly illegal at a time like this. That meant there was nothing here that could draw the law down on him.

She continued to sit where she was, interested now in the sheriff's progress. At first he seemed ready to take the Trail upward into the high country. Then he turned downward as if he had had enough riding through rough country for one day, and he came southward instead.

It struck her suddenly that she could sit here no longer. Soon Sim would meet Griff there on the valley floor and then he would learn that she, too, was out riding. It would not take him long to realize what she was doing away from town. And once that happened, he would do everything he could to stop her from finding Carr.

And now, she knew, she must not only find him to tell him that Sim was riding again, but she must tell him what Griff was doing. She put spurs to her pony, riding dangerously against the oncoming flow of Griff's cattle.

When she reached the road to Carr's place, she turned off. She was almost into the rear yard when she became aware of a man standing, apparently idle, by the kitchen door. He held a carbine cradled under one arm.

She called out her name and when he recognized her, he eased the gun down. But he still stood stiffly, watchfully.

'Just riding, Miss Elsa?'

'I'm not my brother,' she said almost sharply. She stopped the horse and looked down at him. 'I'm trying to find Carr,' she said.

'Sim is riding again and—have you seen what Griff is doing?'

'Bill Marcus went and took a look,' Milo said. He relaxed now. 'Carr's all right. He was in last night—like I said when I saw the sheriff this morning.'

'All right for last night, but what about today?' She told him about Griff's visit in the early afternoon. 'And,' she added, 'what about Ogle and his men? Can I get to the high country along the west ridge?'

'They're still hanging around,' Milo said. 'But they ain't on L-in-C land any more.' He made a disgusted sound. 'They're so danged busy watching for Carr and watching us, I doubt if they've got close enough to the valley to know what's going on.'

'How can I get through?' she demanded urgently.

'Why,' he said, 'ride along the side of the west ridge. Why should Ogle stop you? Tell him you're just following your brother.'

'And if he should stop me . . .'

'There ain't no other way, unless you go through the valley or try a wide swing east up beyond snow line.'

Ogle was a stubborn man, a suspicious man, and she gave him little credit for judgment at a time like this. Yet she saw no other alternative but to follow Milo Carter's suggestion. Lifting a hand to Carter, she swung her horse westward and rode from the yard.

She followed the trail through L-in-C timber, knowing that she was on Ogle's land when she passed a cattle guard on the trail and saw the line of wire fencing running on either side of her, following the irregular line of trees.

Her anxiety to get to Carr whittled away her caution and she was almost to the clump of firs at the junction when she became aware that someone was following her.

She realized her own foolishness then. They were following as carefully as they might, hoping that she would lead them to Carr. Now she dropped her pace. The hoofbeats behind her slowed as well.

In sudden decision, she raked her heels into her horse's flanks, sending him spurting forward. But even as she felt the surge of power and speed flow into her horse, she could hear the swift pounding of a heavier, faster horse behind.

A glance back showed her that the rider was catching her easily. She recognized Ogle, and she could see fury and anger mixed with doubt in his expression.

Then she caught a glimpse of a rider bearing down from the north. Her first thought was that she had been trapped, and then Ogle was alongside her and she turned to him.

He put out one large hand, reaching for her bridle. The movement angered her. 'What right have you to stop me?' she cried at him

'You're going to Carr!' he said accusingly.

'Have you seen what Griff is doing to your valley?' she flung at him. 'Or does it matter to you?'

She saw bewilderment on his face and then it washed away into suspicion. 'Go see for yourself!' she said, and spurted her horse again. He bolted forward, leaving Ogle behind momentarily. To talk to the man was hopeless. Her only chance lay in outrunning him.

But Ogle's horse caught hers easily and this time Ogle tcught the bridle when he reached. Elsa's horse bucked at the sudden pressure and she pitched to one side. Reaching to steady herself, her hand knocked against the butt of the carbine sticking out of its boot. As she straightened, she drew the carbine with her, twisted it to get a grip on the barrel, and then swung toward Ogle. She jabbed the gun butt into Ogle's face, putting all of her strength behind the blow.

Ogle took the blow alongside the jaw. His hands went up in the air, losing their grip on the bridle. She saw him teeter in the saddle briefly and then go sprawling out of it.

Ahead, she could see the other man, and suddenly she realized that it was Carr. Her eyes traveled past him, catching a flicker of movement. Sunlight glinted on metal and she could make out a man standing on the west ridge, steadying himself for a shot at Carr.

She shouted and pointed, trying to stop her galloping horse at the same time. She saw Carr turn and look and then turn back and put his horse into a weaving run. The crack of a rifle echoed in her ears. And as she managed to halt her horse, she looked at Carr's horse and saw it running free, leaving him sprawled on the ground.

She raised the carbine still in her hand, drew a fine bead and fired. The man on the ridge showed surprise; his arms went up and out, the gun falling from his hand, and his body pitched over a sheer drop and she lost sight of it.

Carr stirred as she knelt beside him. She saw the thin line of blood along his neck where the bullet had grazed and she realized that the fall had probably done more damage than the shot. Breathing a prayer of hope, she lifted his head gently.

He opened his eyes. There was a film over them and he looked at her with complete blankness. Then this faded and she knew he saw her. He smiled. Then the smile went away as quickly as had the film over his eyes.

'Ogle—' he began.

'I probably hurt him badly,' she said. 'And I shot that man on the ridge.' The realization of what she had done came to her as she spoke and her eyes widened. 'Carr—'

He lifted a hand and touched her face. 'I thank you,' he said. 'Whether your brother will or not, I don't know.'

Elsa put her head down, touching her lips to his. Then she rose and helped him to his feet. He stood swaying a moment and then nodded that he was all right.

'Groggy, but that's all,' he said. 'My horse . . .'

She found it for him, grazing with Ogle's animal. She rounded them both up and when Carr was in the saddle, they went together to where Ogle lay.

He was still unconscious, a trickle of blood coming from the corner of his mouth where her gun had struck him. Carr got slowly to the ground and knelt to make an examination.

'He's breathing easily enough,' he said. 'But we'll need some water for him.'

Elsa found a canteen on Ogle's saddle and brought it. Carr poured a few drops into Ogle's slack mouth, then a few more. Ogle's throat muscles convulsed as he swallowed. Carr poured the remainder of the water on his face and waited. Ogle's shallow breathing changed and he struggled as if to sit up. Drawing the gun from Ogle's holster, Carr stood and stepped back.

Ogle came to complete consciousness slowly, getting to his feet and standing there for some time before he was fully aware of the situation. And then, when he could focus his eyes, he saw Carr, and this seemed to bring him fully awake.

Elsa spoke first, the words tumbling from her as she addressed Ogle. 'I asked before if you've been to the valley—if you've seen what Griff is doing there?'

'Ah,' Carr said. 'You know that too.'

'I was coming to tell you,' she said. 'And to let you know that Sim is up and riding. He's probably in the valley now.'

Once more suspicion thickened Ogle's expression. Carr said to him, 'And I was looking for you, Mort. To tell you what Griff is up to. You can believe that or not as you wish.'

Ogle's hand pawed at his empty holster and then dropped futilely to his side. 'You hold all the cards now,' he said hoarsely. 'But by God . . .'

'Why should I lie to you? Go and see for yourself.' Carr broke Ogle's gun, emptied it, and handed it over. 'Go take a look, Mort. Then if you still feel the same way, come and get me. I'm up by the Bowl at the head of Rustler's Trail.'

Ogle was silent and Carr laughed into the silence. 'Come and see two hundred head of Griff's cattle that we've taken out of the valley—and go look at the two thousand and more he's driving in there.'

Ogle said thickly, 'I come—and ride into a trap.'

'Think what you will,' Carr said angrily. He turned and walked to his horse, climbing slowly into the saddle. He could feel the sting

131

along his neck where the sniper's bullet had grazed him but more he could feel the pain in his rib cage and he knew that this last fall had done him no good.

Elsa mounted and swung alongside him. Carr turned and glanced at Ogle. He had mounted and was riding slowly back toward the fir trees, sitting carefully in the saddle, both hands clasped over the horn, his head down as if he were thinking.

Elsa said, 'What if he brings a crew—and Sim—up there?'

'Why hasn't he before? He couldn't help knowing where we are. But we're stronger than he, and he knows it. No, he won't come that way. But if he looks at the valley first,' he went on, 'I think he'll come—and he'll be friendly. And we need him, Elsa. We're hamstrung up there, hunted from three sides. Ogle is a gamble I had to make.'

She saw the sudden weariness tighten the skin over his cheekbones. He swayed and would have fallen from the saddle had he not grasped the horn firmly. She rode closer to him, ready in case he should lose his strength again.

'We're going back up there now,' she said. 'Can you ride?'

'I can ride,' he said.

They started northward, going slowly. Carr stopped when he was at a point directly across from where the man on the ridge had been.

They turned, riding toward the ridge, seeking some sight of the man.

Elsa found him and called to Carr, who was searching a short distance away. When he came, he looked only briefly at the limp, broken form sprawled out at the foot of the high drop which led up to the ridge at this point.

'He's one of Griff's men,' Carr said somberly as they rode away. He remembered him as the dish-faced guard who had foolishly lit the cigarette two nights ago. 'His name was Lefty, I think. I'll let Griff know where to find him.'

They rode in silence. The trail was empty and finally they went through the cut and stopped near the entrance to the Bowl. Carr could see Ned Watts perched up above in the rocks and he rode a bit farther to where trees shielded them.

'You took a risk coming to warn me,' he said.

'I had to,' she answered. 'There's no arguing with Sim. I tried. I was very foolish, Carr, and now he suspects me.' She told him what she had said to her brother.

He listened in tight-lipped silence. 'He wouldn't hesitate to jail you,' he said. 'And if that happens . . .'

They were standing beside their horses now. She put out a hand, touching Carr's arm. 'If he does, you'll do nothing.' She dropped her reins and stepped to him, her eyes fixed on his face. 'Don't fight him, Carr. If he's forced, he'll shoot.'

'Ah,' he murmured. 'If I killed your brother . . .'

'Then I don't know,' she said honestly. 'He is my brother, Carr, and he raised me.' She tried with her voice to let him know what was in her mind and heart that she could not put into words. 'He cannot be this way always. Someday his eyes will open.' Her voice dropped, stumbled. 'He's a fine man, Carr—except that he's blinded by the idea of law.'

Carr said, 'Or if he should kill me?'

'I don't know,' she said again. She lifted her eyes and looked into his face searchingly. 'I could ask you to take me now and we could go away. We could start over somewhere, together.' Before he could answer, she rushed on, 'But that is impossible, Carr. I wouldn't ask you to give up what you've done, to abandon your friendship with Pat Tyler, to—'

'And if I were willing?'

She shook her head at the complexity of her own emotions. 'Then, in time I'd probably come to hate you—as you would hate yourself.'

'We'll talk no more about going or about your brother,' he said decisively. 'Except—if he threatens you and you can get away—come to me.' He pointed to the two larch trees ahead. 'Turn left there. Through a bank of buckbrush, there's a small canyon.'

He watched her ride off, and then turned, leading his horse to the canyon.

CHAPTER TEN

Ogle rode slowly along the trail that would lead him to the Saddle. He did not even realize he was at Carr's ranch until he heard the cold, steady voice of Milo Carter.

'Turn around and head back, Ogle. Or you want a bullet in the brisket?'

Ogle lifted his head and saw Milo standing on the rear porch, carbine in his hands. 'I'm going to look at the valley,' Ogle said. His mouth hurt when he talked and he chose his words carefully. 'Carr said for me to.'

'When did you see Carr?' Milo demanded.

'Back there by the firs. He's with the Nash woman. He came riding to tell me something about Griff.'

Milo considered and then lowered the gun. 'Go on,' he said. 'See it for yourself.' He leaned against a porch post and stuffed a pipe with rough-cut tobacco. His eyes followed Ogle, who moved along slowly as if he might be hurt somehow.

'Wonder if seeing that'll sink into his thick head,' Milo murmured. 'I doubt it,' he said clearly aloud, and struck a match to his pipe.

Ogle kept on. He was almost to the wagon

road before he saw the cattle flowing along it. He stopped and studied them for a moment and then turned in the direction of their flow and let them carry him toward the Saddle. There, he pulled aside as Elsa had done, sitting on a slight slope while he looked down into the valley.

'By God,' he whispered. 'By God.'

He saw Griff below talking to two other men, and after a moment of considering, he put his horse back into the stream of cattle and rode there. He stopped facing Griff.

'What is the meaning of this?'

Griff sat with both hands cupped over the horn of his saddle. The two men, both of whom Ogle remembered vaguely as having seen before, grinned a little and moved to one side. Watching them, Ogle realized that he was flanked. He looked again at Griff, waiting for an answer.

'The sheriff asked the same question a while ago,' Griff said easily. 'I'll give you the same answer. I'm just putting some of my beef on here too.'

'This is Government graze—free land,' Ogle said. He spoke slowly because his mouth hurt and because suddenly he felt unsure of himself.'

'So it is,' Griff agreed. 'And there's no law saying how many cattle a man can put on it.'

Ogle pointed to where the men worked, running cattle into the fenced neck of land at the northeast end. 'But you're pushing ours out.

'Hardly,' Griff said. 'They're in there, safe enough.'

'In there? How much grass will they get in there?'

Griff stopped smiling and his voice changed. 'Don't be a fool, Ogle. It happens that I own the Saddle now. And I need all the grass for my beef. I don't care what you do with yours. Let them starve. It's not my worry. But in three days I'm closing the Saddle to public trespass. You'll find a notice posted in town to that effect. If your beef isn't out of here by then, you'll have to do the best you can with them where they are.'

It took a moment for the whole of the pattern to sink into Ogle's mind. Then his eyes went slowly around the steep slopes of the valley, entered only by narrow trails at distant intervals which a man and horse found difficult, and certainly trails too steep for a herd of beef to follow. At the far end there was the broad slash of Rustler's Trail, of course. But it led nowhere as far as driving stock was concerned.

'I'll have the law—' he began.

'What is illegal about closing off my own land to trespass, Ogle?'

For a moment Ogle felt a surge of desire to draw his gun and face Griff down, to wipe the faintly mocking smile from the craggy face.

137

But even as his hand moved, the two men on either side of him touched their gun butts. Ogle let his hand drop to his side. He sat his saddle, shrinking a little, remembering that his own gun was empty.

'Carr was right,' he said wonderingly. 'You tricked Tyler into something. And we were blockheads enough to let Tindle talk us into—' He stopped, his eyes caught by the faint flicker of a smile on Griff's lips. 'We were fools.'

Griff laughed outright. 'You're no less one right now, Ogle.'

Ogle swung his horse about and lashed at its flanks with his spurs. At the top of the Saddle he forced himself to slow down, letting his horse get its wind back, and then he rode on to Purvis' house. Together they got Jerry Dyke, who was sleeping in preparation for a night watch, and then went on to town.

Nash was in bed, the ride having sapped more of his strength than he had expected. He went to the door at Ogle's knock, leading the men into his bedroom where he lay down again.

His voice, when he spoke, was tired. 'You've come about Griff?'

'What right has he to take the valley?' Ogle cried at him.

'Has he taken it?' Nash asked. 'I questioned him about that. Your cattle are still there.'

'And if they're not out in three days,' Ogle cried, 'then we can't get them out. He owns the Saddle.'

'What can the law do? Griff is within his rights stopping trespass on the Saddle.'

'It ain't right!' Larry Purvis cried.

'Maybe not morally,' Nash said, 'but legally he is.'

'By God,' Ogle cried. 'Tyler told us and Carr told us and—'

'When Griff does something illegal, I can act,' Nash said. 'Until he does, there is nothing to be done. Good day, gentlemen.'

Ogle stared down at him, his face reddening. 'Until he does? Can't your law prevent as well as—'

'Like preventing a lynching?' Nash asked quietly. He lay back as Ogle turned about and stomped from the house. Purvis and Dyke followed more quietly.

At the Buckhorn, the three stood at the bar, staring dazedly at one another. Ogle gulped his whiskey blindly, scarcely knowing that he was drinking it.

'By God—'

'Shut up,' Purvis said surprisingly. 'What we got to do is figure something crooked Griff has done.'

'And then what good would the law be? We need an army.' Ogle glared from one to the other. 'We'll push him out.'

'A range war?' Jerry Dyke asked softly. 'What will that solve?'

Ogle turned on him, his face flushed. 'You

139

want to lose that grass? You want to stand by and see him gobble it and then gobble the Bunchgrass—the whole country?'

'No,' Dyke admitted. 'But what good are a few of us against the men he can get? Where do we get this army to push him out with?'

Ogle's hand lifted as if to point somewhere. Then it fell to his side. 'By God,' he muttered. It was all he could say.

*   *   *

That night after supper, Ogle sat in his parlor, watching his wife work on the quilt. It was the first time in so long that he had been home except to eat that being there felt strange. He sat trying to think, trying to twist and turn his mind that was essentially straightforward into a pattern that would find the crookedness in Neil Griff.

He thought back to what Griff had said there in the valley, and suddenly he fastened onto one thing—a small thing. He recalled the expression on Griff's face when he had mentioned Tindle. The slight flicker of Griff's superior smile came before his eyes sharply. Drawing a deep breath, he sat motionless for a moment, his hands clasped over his knees, his head bowed.

Then he rose, buckled on his gun, and started for the door. His wife looked up from her sewing. 'Going again? I had hoped this business was done.'

'Not yet,' he said shortly. As an afterthought, he went back and kissed her goodbye.

Outside, he saddled and rode for Tindle's. Although Griff owned the land now, Ogle knew that Tindle had stayed there. It was a small place, hidden in the scrub timber on the west side, not too far from the L-in-C.

Ogle rode through the thin moonlight, trying to piece together what he must say and do. He had to overcome the great shame in himself for the way he had acted before he could get his mind clear enough to function at all. But at last he had it straight and he stepped up the pace of his horse.

He found Tindle alone, lying on his bunk with a whiskey bottle beside him, his shattered arm bandaged in a splint. He showed bad teeth in a grin of welcome when the door opened and he saw that it was Ogle.

'Going after Tyler again?' He smelled of stale whiskey and sweat and unwashed bedclothes. The close little room was fetid with the odor and it took Ogle a moment to adjust himself to it after the freshness of the night outside.

He stood silently, his back against the closed door, and Tindle went on, 'I ain't ready, but when you get ahold of that Lindon, let me know. I got a score to settle with him.'

Ogle moved then, crossing the room to the

bunk in short, choppy strides. The grin went off Tindle's face as Ogle reached out and jerked him forward, slapping him across the face with a heavy hand.

'Almighty!' Tindle pulled away and clawed frantically beneath his filthy pillow. He came up with a gun.

Ogle reached out and struck Tindle's hand with the side of his fist. The gun fell to the floor alongside the bunk. Ogle left it there, drew his own gun, and raked the sight down Tindle's cheek. Tindle whimpered and squeezed back against the wall.

Acting this way was a new thing to Ogle and for a moment the sight of the blood that oozed from the scratch on Tindle's face stopped him. Then he lifted the gun again. 'Griff hired you,' he said in a dull voice.

'What you talking about? What's got into you?'

Ogle stared down at him, sickened by the frightened manner in which Tindle crouched back against the wall. He lowered the gun and stepped back. Finding a chair, he drew it forward and sat down. He aimed the gun at Tindle, not as a club this time but with the sight pointed for the man's face. He cocked the gun, making a loud, deadly sound in the stillness.

'Griff hired you to stir us up,' he said. 'To lead us to Tyler that noon. Nothing happened until you came in to it.'

'You're crazy, Ogle.'

Ogle moved the gun so that he could look down the barrel. He held his position, watching the sweat break out on Tindle. He saw the man's fear rise, saw the pallor of terror spread across his features.

Tindle made a whimpering sound and tried to press harder against the wall. Ogle kept the gun steady, not moving, not taking his eyes from Tindle's face.

'You been talking to Lindon, Ogle?' the frightened little man said, his voice shaking and finally breaking upward into a shriek. 'What got into you? You gone crazy?'

Ogle waited with all the vast patience that was in him now that he had this thought out and knew what he must do.

Tindle stared at the gun, and a trickle of saliva ran out of one corner of his mouth and down the stubble on his chin. He started to speak again and then lay there, gasping for air. There was no movement, no sign from Ogle except the motionless gun in his hand.

Tindle broke. 'You're right! You're right!'

Ogle lowered his arm, resting the gun gently on his leg. 'So we were tricked,' he whispered. 'Was that Tyler—that noon you led us up Rustler's Trail?'

Tindle pulled himself away from the wall and reached for the whiskey bottle. He got it to his lips and worried the cork out with his teeth and spat it aside. When he drank, his teeth rattled on the neck. He took the bottle away and blew his breath gustily.

'It was one of Griff's men.'

'Which one?'

'I don't know,' Tindle said. He saw the gun that was resting on Ogle's leg begin to rise. The fear was still deep inside him and it made his words burst out as if he were eager to get rid of them. 'Put that gun away. I'll tell you all I know.'

Ogle let the muzzle of the gun drop so that it was aimed at the floor. 'Go on.'

'I was told to get you up to the valley right after noon dinner.'

'Where was Tyler?'

'Up in the hills with one of Griff's men.'

'Who?' Ogle's voice was without expression, but the very emptiness of it was a threat in Tindle's ears.

'The heavy-set one—named Dutch.'

Ogle nodded. He recalled him as one of the pair who had flanked him in the valley that afternoon. 'And the other? The one we thought was Tyler?'

'Big blond man—name of Perly.'

Ogle nodded again. That would be the other one he had seen with Griff today in the valley. 'And the night the sheriff was shot— what about that?'

'I don't know,' Tindle said. 'All I know is that Griff said Nash wouldn't stop us. I was supposed to hold the lynching until Dutch showed up.'

'Ah,' Ogle murmured, 'so he could kill Nash and have us blamed for it.'

'Yeah,' Tindle said. He licked his lips. 'I suppose it was like that.' He fell silent, sitting with the bottle upright, its thick base resting on his stomach.

The gun lifted again. He struggled to sit up straighter, and some of the whiskey slopped from the neck of the bottle. 'That's all I know. I swear it!'

Ogle kept the gun coming because he did not know what else to do. All the things Carr had said to him came flooding back, making his face flush with the shame of what he had done. He looked at Tindle and saw him as a symbol of wrongness. He kept the gun moving until it pointed at Tindle's belly.

'I don't know any more. I swear. I—'

'Get up,' Ogle said. 'We're going to town.'

Tindle started to swing his legs over the side of the bunk and then, with a scream of tortured rage, threw the bottle at Ogle and rolled off the bed at the same time.

Ogle lifted an arm and felt the jar of the bottle against it. There was the stink of spilled liquor mixed with the shrilling of Tindle's frightened shrieks. Ogle stood up, kicking the chair away.

Tindle was on the floor, his hand on the gun Ogle had knocked there. He brought the gun around, thumbing back the hammer awkwardly as he did so. The shot went wide and he brought the gun to bear more steadily on Ogle. As the first shot thundered through the stinking confusion of the cabin, Ogle shot, and another explosion rocketed painfully within the walls of the tiny cabin. He stared in surprise as Tindle fell backward, hit the side of the bunk, and rolled to the floor and over onto his back. The bullet had struck Tindle in the face.

Ogle holstered his gun and turned and walked out. He stood just outside the door, sucking the freshness of the night air into his lungs, letting it still the shaking within him. It struck him that he had killed a man—a thing he had never done or thought to do, even in self-defense. He had let Carr run over him that night of Tyler's escape because he had not been able to shoot. Now he had killed a man.

He was halfway home when he realized that he had done more. Tindle's death had pushed his preconceived plan out of his head. 'By God,' he whispered aloud. 'By God!' He had killed the witness he needed, the man he had planned to take to Nash. He had killed the proof that would have forced Nash to believe that Griff was a threat to the ranchers' further existence.

CHAPTER ELEVEN

Sheriff Nash lay in bed and listened to Elsa moving quietly about the house. He had been awake when she had ridden in the afternoon before, shortly after Ogle and his friends had left. The flush on her face, the excitement lighting her eyes, had told him that she had seen Carr Lindon. Tired as he was, he had done nothing. Nor, he knew, could he do more without definite proof.

When she finally came in to him, she was dressed in her jeans and flannel shirt. She stopped just inside the door, looking to see if he was awake or asleep. When he looked at her, she said, 'I'm going riding. Sim. Is there anything I can do before I leave?'

'Nothing. I'm all right. This day's rest has done me good.'

She was silent a moment. Then she said, 'You saw what Griff was doing in the valley yesterday?'

'I saw.'

'Don't his actions mean anything to you? Don't they prove that what Carr says is true, Sim?'

'They prove nothing of the sort,' he said. His voice sharpened as it always did at the mention of Carr. 'Perhaps they will. Griff may overstep himself. Until then—what has he done that I could accuse him of on legal grounds?'

She stood mute a moment and then turned away. 'I'll be back in time to cook supper,' she said.

'No need, I'm all right now,' he said. He lay listening to her footsteps, the soft closing of the rear door. Then he threw back the covers and stood up. He had remained in bed since yesterday afternoon and now the motion of standing made him momentarily dizzy. When that passed, he dressed quickly and went outside. His horse saddled, he mounted and rode north.

When he reached the foot of theswitchback, he could see her ahead, following the zigzag of the trail, maintaining a steady upward pace. When she had disappeared over the top, he sent his horse after her. Even so, when he reached the top, he could still see her some distance ahead, riding at the same steady pace.

At the junction marked by the fir trees, he noted that she had continued ahead, taking the trail that led to the high country by way of the west ridge.

Now he stopped following her and turned off, cutting across Ogle's land and working his way up to the south end of the ridge along a narrow path that was little more than a deer track in many places. It was a difficult trip for a horse and more than once he had to stop and lead the animal up sheer pitches. At the top, he was forced to lie down and rest unfit the trembling in his muscles quieted enough to let him climb into the saddle.

The ridge itself was easy enough riding, although he kept dangerously close to the west edge in the hope that he could avoid being seen from down in the valley. Finally he was stopped by a sheer drop that looked northeastward to the top of Rustler's Trail and the Bowl. He had been screened there for some time by a thin growth of timber, and thinking that Carr might have a lookout posted somewhere near the Bowl, he left his horse and stayed well within the trees.

Looking to his right and downward, he could see the tiny figures that were Griff and his men running Leaning-G beef about the valley. The drive had stopped and now the men were working to spread the great herd over the graze more evenly. In the far distance, Nash could make out the movements of men who were still putting the others' cattle behind the temporary fence at the northeast end. He frowned. In his own mind, he sympathized with Mort Ogle and his friends. But sympathy had not written the law and so Nash felt helpless. His own futility made him irritable.

He watched Elsa come out of the cut near the Bowl, go across its mouth and ride directly toward two larch trees that he could barely see from where he sat. Then she disappeared.

He waited patiently until she came into

night again. This time she was not alone. Without being able to see the man clearly, Nash knew that it was Carr Lindon. They stopped for a moment near the entrance to the cut, within range of his vision but off from anyone else's by the timber behind them.

They talked for some time, standing beside their horses, and then they embraced for, what seemed to Nash, quite a long time. After that she mounted her pony and rode away with no more ceremony than a lift of her hand. Carr, he noticed, sat looking in the direction she had gone for a while before he turned about. Then he rode quickly, past the mouth of the Bowl, straight to the larch trees, and then disappeared.

Sim Nash drew farther back to where his horse waited. He had a heavy sheepskin-lined coat tied to his saddle and a bit of food in his saddlebag. He sat, huddled in the greatcoat, and ate his sandwich of bread and beef, washing it down with sips of water from his canteen. The sun had gone behind the distant western ridges and the air at this altitude was suddenly chilly. The valley below was rapidly being swallowed by the shadows of evening and the men had all disappeared, leaving nothing but the restless cattle.

Having eaten, Nash returned to his original lookout and sat until darkness fell. Then he backtracked until there was a place where he could lead his horse down to the trail. From there he rode to the small cut, where he dismounted, tied the horse, and walked the rest of the way on foot.

He had no way of knowing if there was a lookout posted here, nor where the man might be. But he had done this sort of thing too many times before not to exercise every precaution, and so he moved forward testing every step, judging every shadow as he went.

Once be was startled by the voices of two men and he drew into a screen of bushes until they passed. He recognized Pat Tyler and old Peak by their voices. They went within six feet of him, swinging a deer carcass from a pole. Then they disappeared into the darkness ahead.

When he saw that the moon was about to rise, he eased forward until he was beside the larch trees. Now he could only stand and look about in the darkness, baffled by the lack of sound, or sign of anyone near by. It was almost by accident that he saw the faintest glimmer of the fire that led him to them.

He crept up to the screen of buckbrush and timber and found that, by moving to one side of the place where it had obviously been tramped, he could see beyond it. Now he could make out the narrow canyon mouth with the overhang, just inside it. He saw three men squatted around the fire. They were eating supper and talking, and he had to work himself farther toward them before he could catch

151

anything of what they were saying. Even then, it was difficult.

Carr said, 'I expected to see Ogle before this.'

Pat Tyler answered something that was drowned by the crackle of the fire, and Carr's voice came again. 'I'll stake what I've got that he and Purvis and Dyke will be along. They need us now as much as we need them.'

Nash strained to hear more. But Peak rose and threw another stick of dry pine on the fire, making it crackle and pop, and for some time he could catch nothing but the occasional lift of a man's voice. Finally the fire quieted. Pat Tyler was on his feet, moving about in his restless fashion.

'When do we go?' he demanded suddenly.

Carr's answer was clear and decisive. 'As soon as we know we'll get help from Ogle.'

'And if we don't?'

Nash could not hear the answer. But he did not need it.

He backed away, more cautiously than he had advanced. The fourth man—it would be Ned Watts, he thought—must be on guard somewhere nearby. And now, though a sudden urgency drove him, he wanted less than ever to be discovered.

He reached his horse finally, but for the sake of caution led it until he was well onto the flat. Then he mounted and rode fast for town. Even so, it was late when he arrived.

Despite the fact that he felt Ogle and the others to be morally justified in their desire to drive Griff away, there was no confusion in Nash's mind as to his course of action.

He did not like the action that lay ahead of him, but he could see no other course. The law was made by man to control men. To break the law, therefore, was the greatest of sins in the eyes of Sim Nash. To preserve it, he had killed more than one man, taken more than one bullet himself, chanced his life more times than he cared to remember.

He left his horse saddled, went to his office and made some preparations, and then walked slowly to the house. Elsa was in the parlor sewing buttons on one of his shirts. When he came in, she left her work and went to the kitchen.

'Your supper is in the oven, Sim.'

She watched him sit down with the carefulness of a man weary in body and mind. She set the food before him and then stood back. 'Is it wise for you to be up so much, Sim?'

'I had business.' He bent to his food, taking it in quick, gulping bites, hardly seeming to chew before he swallowed. The urgency was still strong within him, yet he knew that he had to eat to have strength enough for the night ahead.

Elsa returned to her work, leaving him alone. When he was through eating, he smoked a cigarette, turning over in his mind again and again this plan he had formed. He hoped that he could find some other way but there was none that he could see. At last he went to the parlor and stood before her, his face stern.

'I tracked you,' he said in a bleak voice. 'I saw you ride to Lindon. You took food to him today.'

'So I did,' she admitted quietly. She laid aside her sewing and stood up. 'Now you have proof, haven't you?'

'I have no proof that you helped Tyler escape, though now I believe you when you said you did. But I have proof that you're helping criminals to hide. You, the sister of the sheriff. If you cannot respect the law, who can?'

'Don't lecture me, Sim. I go by my heart and my head. You go by that cold knot you call your "reason."' She faced him, her head lifted. 'Do as you wish, but don't waste your time trying to make me believe there is any justice in your law.'

'Get your things,' he said. 'I've fixed a cell for you.'

She showed no surprise that he actually meant to put her in jail. Quietly she walked from the room to her own. She had changed from her riding clothes and they, with her gun and belt, hung in the closet. She went to it, opened the door, and stepped inside. When she came out, she wore the riding clothes and the .38 was in her hand.

She started for the door and then noticed that he stood just inside it. He had been waiting, his own gun in his hand. He simply looked at her until she turned away and replaced the gun and holster in the closet.

'I'm ready, Sim,' she said.

Silent still, he led her to the jail and put her inside the end cell and closed the door. The sound of the lock clicking shut put a cold, hard knot of anguish in his stomach. He walked away, not looking back.

* * *

Nash took the wagon road that led to the Saddle. He was going to see Neil Griff. Though he did not relish the idea of asking the man for assistance, he knew that it was his only choice. He did not expect Griff to be able to help him take Carr without a fight and he had deliberately taken care of the problem of Elsa first in order that he would be assured she was out of any possible danger.

He had studied the idea of asking for help elsewhere. There was no longer the possibility of getting aid from Ogle, whether or not he joined Carr. Nash knew this without any conscious reasoning; he had met men like Ogle before and always they were as dogmatic about a new belief as about an old one. To recruit men from saloons, men he had arrested before and might have to arrest again, had crossed his mind but he had rejected it almost instantly. Carr Lindon was no one to be taken lightly, he knew. It would require skilled fighters, and he was sure Griff's men were just that.

He turned into the road that led to the Leaning-G. When Nash was close enough to see the light shining from the house, a man stepped into the road, a rifle cradled in his arms.

'Nash here,' he said quickly.

'We don't need the law,' the man said.

'I came to see Griff.' Nash felt a chill anger at the man's insolence but he kept his temper under control. It struck him as curious that Griff would feel the need of a watchman. Unless, he thought, Griff had a way of knowing that Carr Lindon planned an attack on him. And if this were true, why had he not come to the law with his information?

Nash kept moving forward toward the guard and finally he raised the rifle, aiming at Nash's torso. Nash reined in and waited now, while the man appeared to be trying to decide whether or not to let him by. Shortly he became tired of this and started his horse forward again. The rifle did not move nor did the man.

Nash said, 'I want to see Griff,' and moved the reins so that he went to one side of the guard. The rifle pushed upward, threateningly. That was the man's mistake, Nash thought. He pulled the reins the other way suddenly, making his horse step toward the guard. As the man backed off, Nash reached out and got the rifle barrel and jerked. The rifle came free and he laid it across his lap.

'I said I wanted to see Griff! Move!'

The man swore at him thickly, but he walked ahead, his hands extended slightly from his sides. When they reached the veranda, the door opened and Griff came out. He looked puzzled as Nash leaned from the saddle and handed the rifle to him.

'This belongs to your man, Griff. You should teach him some manners.'

'Did you come to criticize my help or to see me?' Griff asked in an amused voice. He took the rifle and tossed it contemptuously to the waiting man.

'Go on back, Perly.'

Nash watched the man walk off truculently. He was big and blond and when he walked in that fashion he reminded Nash of Pat Tyler. He turned back to Griff.

'What do you need a guard for?'

'I'm cautious,' Griff said easily. 'Ogle doesn't like what I'm doing. And somebody killed one of my men yesterday—Lindon or Ogle, I suppose. He was found in the valley this morning. He had been carried there from the look of things.'

'Why wasn't I told?'

Griff had a ready answer. 'I'm not casual, Sheriff. I'm just controlled. And why should I bring more trouble to you when you're obviously still ill? I can handle my own affairs.'

'Not legally.'

'If they come on my property, yes. Do I look like I'm riding out to take the law into my own hands?' He seemed impatient suddenly. 'What was it you wanted, Sheriff?'

'I came to ask your help. I want to get Lindon and the others.'

'Then I can take the law into my hands?' Griff asked. His voice was tinged with amusement.

'You'll ride as my deputies,' Nash said. 'I want no shooting except in self-defense.'

'As a good citizen, I can hardly refuse my services,' Griff said. 'How many men do you want?'

'What can you spare?'

'Six, couting myself. That will make seven of us, Sheriff. Do we go now?'

'When you're ready.' Nash said.

'Come in and warm yourself while I get the men together,' Griff said. He waited for Nash to get off his horse and then held the door for him. Nash sat in the parlor alone while Griff went to the bunkhouse. He came back shortly and took a bottle from a cupboard. 'Let me give you a drink, Sheriff. It will be a cold night.'

Nash took the drink and downed it quickly. He was grateful for the temporary energy it gave him. He said, 'What is this about your man, Griff?'

Griff shrugged. 'He was one of those who was attacked the other night guarding my beef. I suppose being knocked out got under his skin and he went looking for Lindon. All I know is that we found him in the valley this morning. He was shot with a carbine.'

Griff talked too easily, let it slip out too smoothly, Nash felt. But there was nothing he could point to and say, 'This is wrong.' He sat silent, turning this over in his mind, wondering about it. And wondering too if it had been such a good idea to ask Griff for help.

Then a voice called from outside and they rose. 'Time to ride,' Griff said. He poured a second drink. 'To success,' he said, lifting his glass. 'May Lindon and Tyler be in jail by dawn, Sheriff.'

Nash drank with him and then walked to the door without speaking.

CHAPTER TWELVE

Ogle spent the day after Tindle's death riding the hills, turning over and over in his mind what he had done and what he must do. His impulse was to go to Nash and tell him what

159

Tindle had said. But he knew that he would be asked to produce the man and then he would have to admit that he had shot him. And though Ogle knew it had been in self-defense, how could he convince Nash of that?

Once he turned and rode north into the high country. But his shame at what he had said and done to Carr and Pat Tyler was as great as his self-disgust for having shot Tindle, and he knew that he could not yet face the men hiding up there.

Finally he rode home and ate a quick supper. Then he went out to his veranda to smoke a pipe. He set it aside after a few puffs; there was no peace in him, and he knew there would be none until he had the killing off his conscience and until he had somehow straightened out that which his stubbornness had caused. The knowledge that he might have condemned innocent men to a life of running and hiding lay heavily on him. But he sat until late before he finally moved.

Then he saddled his horse and rode to town, neither hurrying nor lingering. He moved at a steady pace, turning over in his mind what he had to say to Nash and what he should do if Nash refused to believe him.

The house was dark when he went by on the alley side. But there was a light in one of the cells and he decided to go to the office by way of the corridor through the annex. He tried the door and found it locked and was about to go around when a voice called out, halting him. 'Who is it?'

Ogle swung his head in the darkness, not understanding a woman's voice coming from a cell. He said tentatively, 'Miss Elsa?'

'Here.'

Ogle went around to where he could look in the cell window. He saw her standing there, quiet and self-possessed. 'What happened, ma'am?'

When Elsa recognized who it was, the faint flame of hope she had had plummeted. And then a little of the light from the cell struck his face and she saw there something that made her hope rise again.

'My brother put me here,' she said, 'for helping Carr.'

Ogle said nothing and her voice lashed out, bitter with anger at herself for not having fought back against Sim Nash. 'He's out catching Carr and Pat right now. I'm surprised he didn't come to you for help.'

'Not to me,' Ogle said in his heavy way. 'Not to us ranchers. We asked him for help against Griff and got laughed at.' He stood twisting his hat in his hands, wondering if he should not tell this girl his story. She could relay it to Nash for what it was worth. At least it would help Ogle sleep.

He blurted, 'I came because Carr is right, ma'am. I found out from Tindle last night. He told me how Griff fixed it to have us think we

161

saw Tyler rustling—only it was a man named Perly. And how Griff fixed it to keep the sheriff away during the—the lynching. Tindle was paid to rile us up and we was fools enough to go along with him.'

'You were drunk,' she said, offering him salve for his conscience.

'A fool is a fool, drunk or sober,' he said stubbornly.

'But if you bring Tindle in,' she suggested.

He almost tore his big hat with a convulsive movement of his strong fingers. 'He's dead. I shot him. He came at me with a gun and—I shot him.'

She understood what lay now on Ogle's conscience. But that was something he would have to fight out with himself. There was a more pressing matter gnawing at her, and she said, 'Why don't you go to Carr and offer your help? If Sim didn't ask you for help, he must have gone to Griff.'

The implacation of this sank slowly into his mind. 'To Griff?'

'Where else?' she demanded. 'Who else is there for him to turn to? And he knows where Carr is. He told me that he trailed me today.'

Her hands were on the bars, holding them so that her knuckles showed white with the pressure of her grip. 'You could at least warn Carr that Sim knows where he is—that he's coming to arrest them. He hasn't been gone long. And if he stops to get Griff and his men, there'll be time.'

Ogle twisted his hat again and then in sudden decision, jammed it on his head. 'I'll go,' he said. 'I'll go now.' His face showed the pain working within him. 'It's something I can do for them.'

'It's a great deal,' she said softly. 'Hurry!'

She watched him go to his horse, mount, and ride off, his movements deliberate, seemingly slow. If only he would move faster, she thought. Carr had told her today that if he were cornered by her brother, he would fight, and his words still lay heavily on her mind.

'I could do nothing else,' he had said. 'The sheriff is as much our enemy as Griff at a time like this.'

'Hurry,' she whispered into the night after Ogle. 'Hurry!'

* * *

On watch, Carr stood huddled against the cold of the high country. Now and then he had to shift his position to relieve cramped muscles or stamp his feet on the rocks when the cold seeped too deeply through his boots. He had stationed himself at a point just above the mouth of the Bowl.

He first heard the sound from a distance, a clang of metal against rock. He paused in his movements and listened, straining to catch the sound again. It came—fainter this time but closer. He let out the breath he had been holding and it frosted around his face and thinned away in the chill air. The waning moon was highlighting the countryside with a thin brilliance that made every shadow a deep, impenetrable blackness.

Only one rider, he thought, and he wondered if Nash would be fool enough to come here after them alone. Ned Watts, on guard that afternoon, had told them he had spotted Nash riding on the west ridge and that he may have seen them.

Carr moved again as the cold crept deeper into him. There was only one way to determine the identity of the oncoming rider and so he moved down the rocks until he was in shadow at the edge of the trail. The faint creak of saddle leather and the jingling of the bit was close now and he lifted his carbine, readying himself.

A horse appeared in a patch of moonlight not far ahead. He strained to see the rider but the moonlight was deceptive and he could make out only the bulk of a man.

Horse and rider were almost on Carr when he recognized Mort Ogle. and he let his carbine down softly. 'Rein in, Mort,' he called softly.

The horse stopped with a jerk. A heavy sigh gurgled from Ogle as if he had held it deep inside himself for some time 'Carr?'

'Stay where you are.'

'They're coming,' Ogle said in a desperate, husky whisper. 'I think I saw seven coming up the Trail. Nash found your hide-out today and he got Griff to help him.' Carr did not respond, and he added, 'Elsa told me he trailed her today. She's been put in jail for it, Carr.'

Carr stood where he was. He was not surprised at the news about Elsa. It would be like Nash to do just such a thing, even to his own sister. But Griff . . . Then Carr realized that there was no reason yet for Nash not to trust the man. As far as he was concerned, Griff had done nothing wrong.

'Why didn't Nash ask you?" Carr asked pointedly.

'Not me, Carr. What you said—all the things you said—was true enough.'

Carr knew how much it had cost Mort Ogle to say those words, and for the first time he accepted the message as full truth. He started to speak and Ogle held up his hand. In the silence, Carr could hear the scuff of hoofs on rock, the slow movement of laden horses making the last steep pitch to the top of the Trail. From the sounds, Carr judged it to be a good-sized crew.

Carr looked again at Ogle. 'Thanks for the warning,' he said. 'And go back while you can, Mort.'

'I can help,' Ogle said in his stubborn way. 'I got to help, Carr.'

'I want your help,' Carr said quickly. 'But not here. I want you to get Purvis and Jerry Dyke and go to my place. If we get through, we can meet you there.' His voice was low but sharp. 'We have to hit Griff soon, law or no law.'

Ogle nodded as if he had been hoping for this. 'We'll be there,' he said. Then he swung his horse about and rode the other way.

Carr hurried to where he had left his own horse in the timber, mounted, and started for the mouth of the canyon. He was brought up short by the crack of a gunshot. He looked back over his shoulder and he could see Ogle, outlined in the moonlight, riding low in the saddle, weaving as he went across the top of Rustler's Trail. A gun barked again, coming from below Ogle.

Ogle straightened suddenly, a gun in his hand. He fired wildly downward, and then he was gone into the cut.

Carr rode for the canyon, wondering what they could do against seven men. The shots had warned the others and he found them in the saddle when he arrived. He said, 'Nash and Griff's men are coming. Let's ride.'

'Ride where?' Tyler demanded.

'Leave the fire,' Carr said. 'It might hold them for a minute or two. Maybe we can pull into the timber and then get around them.'

'And get boxed?' Tyler said. 'I say stand and fight.'

'We could hold them off all night,' Carr admitted. 'But we'd still be here when day came. And I'll not fight the law until I have to.'

'That may be soon,' Tyler told him dryly. The noise of oncoming riders was close enough now to be heard over the crackle of the fire. 'Sooner,' he added wryly.

Carr took the lead. 'Break for it,' he ordered. 'But stay together.'

They went out of the canyon, crashing through the screen of buckbrush, and turned eastward into the thickest of the darkness.

The sheriff's posse moved up the Trail, with Nash and Griff in the lead. When they were nearly to the top, they could hear the sounds of a horse picking its way over rock a short distance above. Griff spurred forward, topping a low rise. The moonlight showed him the horse and rider and he lifted a hand for the men to come on.

Nash and two of the men arrived at the same time. Before Nash could speak, the rider on his left lifted his gun and fired. The man above bent low and attempted to hurry his horse, going now at a weaving run. There was another shot from beside Nash.

'Hold it, Perly!' It was Nash. Then he ducked to one side as the man above straightened in the saddle, turned, and sent a flurry of shots at them. Beside Nash, Perly made an odd sound in his throat and slid gently from his horse to the ground. Up above, the man cried something at them they could not hear and disappeared westward.

Dutch was alongside Perly, swearing from deep inside himself. 'Perly's hit, Boss. Let me get the—'

'Go ahead,' Griff agreed.

'Wait!' Nash ordered.

'Wait, hell,' Dutch answered. He climbed back on his horse and urged it forward. 'Wait for what—a trial?' He spurred to the top of the Trail, and swung in the direction the rider had taken.'

Griff was laughing at the sheriff. 'What difference does it make how we get them, Nash? A bullet is as settling as a noose, isn't it?'

'I want them taken in for trial,' Nash said coldly.

'Trial? Yesterday Lindon shot one of my men—remember. Did he get a trial?'

Nash realized now how tenuous was the loyalty of these men. And although he was willing to face them individually or collectively to force them to do as he ordered, it was in his mind that finding Carr Lindon and Tyler was the more important thing at the moment.

He did not argue Griff's point. He said, 'They'll be warned now. Let's get there.'

They left Perly with a man to tend him and went on. They were four now, men riding straight in the saddle, alert. At the top they turned for the two larch trees a short way east.

The bursting of a horse through brush popped loudly on the still night air. 'Fan out!' Nash cried. 'Fan out! Don't let them break through.'

They pressed on, not in file now, but the noises ahead stopped abruptly, leaving them with nothing to go by. The faint light of the campfire appeared to their left, and Nash swung his horse in that direction.

'Careful,' he warned. 'They might be trying to get us in there and bottle us up.'

'Then shoot up the place,' Griff said to him. 'What are you waiting for—to make an arrest?'

Nash had his gun out but he made no attempt to bring it up. 'I'm the law. I do this my way.'

Griff turned contemptuously away from him and signaled to his men. Together they charged the growth of brush that screened away all but a flicker of the firelight. At the last moment they swept aside, firing into the narrow mouth of the cut, then turning and sweeping back again. There were no answering shots, no sounds of any kind.

Griff pulled up beside Nash. 'Your birds have flown. This is your country, Sheriff. Maybe you know where they've gone.'

Nash's anger at this insubordination was making him shake, and he had to fight to regain control of himself. He said shortly, 'East is the only way—if they can get through.

169

It's like climbing a cliff face.'

'We can box them,' Griff said. There was an undercurrent of amusement threading his voice. 'Let's ride, boys.'

They moved slowly eastward, Griff letting Nash lead now. There was no sound but that of their own making. The trail narrowed, becoming little more than a deer track. As the cliffs came down toward there, the timber began to disappear, and finally them was nothing but an apparently sheer wall of rock ahead. It rose stark and naked in the moonlight, towering above into the snow and dropping to nothingness below. Nash stopped when there was nowhere else to ride.

Griff spoke for them all. 'They haven't gone past here,' he said. 'How could they have got away?'

'Unless they pulled back into the timber and let us ride past—' Nash began, but stopped abruptly. They could all hear the noise of horses trying to move quietly not far behind them.

'Back!' Griff cried. 'Cut them off!'

He reined about and drove his horse recklessly along the dark, narrow trail. His men pounded after him, and Nash brought up the rear, going more cautiously because he could feel his small store of strength going rapidly.

When the trail was wide enough for four men to ride abreast, Griff stopped and turned.

170

'Fan out again,' he ordered.

They sat with their guns out, blocking any progress westward. Once more the night was quiet. Griff raised his voice almost to a shout, 'Comb that timber!'

'Wait!' It was Nash, but his voice was drowned by the simultaneous roar of three carbines. They fired once, twice, and then stopped.

'All right.' It was Carr's voice coming from not far ahead.

Griff laughed softly. 'Come out with your hands up,' he ordered.

In a moment three men appeared, walking slowly, leading their horses by reins held high, well above the guns on their hips. The fourth man was in the saddle, slumped forward with both hands gripping tightly on the horn. Griff moved forward warily, looking for a trap. But when the rider was close, the blood on his shirt could be seen plainly. It was Pat Tyler and he seemed barely conscious.

'Four?' Nash said questioningly. 'Then who was the one your man rode after, Griff?'

'Maybe it was someone come to warn them, Sheriff,' Griff said mockingly. 'Your sister again?'

Nash answered coldly, 'Elsa is in jail for breaking the law, Griff. She couldn't have been the one.'

Griff laughed openly at him. 'Tyler managed to get out. Lindon is a clever man,

Sheriff. A very clever man.' He looked at the silent group standing. 'But not clever enough,' he added.

CHAPTER THIRTEEN

Ogle heard the sound of the rider behind him when he was still in the cut-off between the Trail and the off side of the west ridge. He urged his horse to more speed, but the animal was tired and Ogle was a heavy man, hard on a mount.

The rider was closing in rapidly and Ogle judged that he would be caught shortly after he broke out of the cut. He rode leaning forward, his breath coming sharply in anger.

When he was nearly to open country, he knew what he must do. Even if the man behind him were the sheriff, he had only one choice. He could not outrun the other—he could only stand and fight.

The cut sprawled open suddenly, precipitating him onto a bench almost barren of trees. Ahead the bench dropped off to a sheer fall. To the right the land sloped up sharply into the mountains, and to the left was the trail toward town. Ogle rode straight ahead until he was forced to stop where the bench went down sharply. Leaving his horse tied to a scrub sapling, he started walking back toward the cut.

The hoofbeats of the oncoming rider's horse grew insistent, rising sharply as they echoed out of the narrow canyon. Suddenly the man came into sight, low in the saddle, riding fast.

Ogle stopped walking and cupped his hands about his mouth. He drew a deep breath and called loudly, 'Here, you!'

The rider reined in so sharply that the horse's front feet pawed for the sky. Then he was level again, straight in the saddle, moonlight glinting on the gun in his hand.

Ogle called again, 'Nash?'

'Nash hell!' the man shouted. He kicked his horse forward, riding straight for Ogle. The distance Ogle estimated to be a hundred yards, and he stood his ground until the man was halfway to him and then he drew.

The rider fired at the motion, but Ogle had shifted his heavy body to one side, seeking to better his target, and the bullet whispered a short distance from his head. He fired now. The other man answered as Ogle moved again, instinctively, shooting as he went.

The rider swore shrilly as a shot took his horse out from under him, catapulting him forward. He struck on his shoulder and side, rolled and came to one knee. He stayed that way, breathing through his mouth as if in pain, facing Ogle, who was now less than twenty yards from him.

'Who is it?' Ogle demanded.

'The horse farmer!' the man cried in surprise.

Ogle recognized Dutch now and sudden exultation rose in him. 'Good,' he said quietly.

'One more step and . . .'

Ogle was puzzled at the tone of the man's voice. Why didn't he shoot? And then Ogle walked forward; and understood. Dutch was on one knee, resting his right arm on the other leg. He was bringing his left hand over, trying to steady his right wrist. By the way it hung, Ogle guessed that Dutch's arm had been broken in his fall.

Ogle continued walking. 'I can't shoot a hurt man. Put down your gun.'

Dutch drew back his lips in a snarl as he tried to force his useless right hand to squeeze the trigger. Ogle came forward steadily, unyielding. Dutch cursed at him shrilly and took the gun in his left hand and fired. The motion was an awkward one, sending the bullet into the dirt at Ogle's feet.

Dutch fired again, and again he missed. Ogle continued to come forward, and when he was close, he stopped and shot. The gun went spinning away, making Dutch cry out at the sudden numbness of his empty hand.

'I couldn't be sure of doing that from any distance,' Ogle said. There was an immense satisfaction in him. He finally had a witness to take to the sheriff. Even though Dutch and

Nash had ridden together this night, Ogle felt that Nash could not deny the truth once he heard it from one of Griff's own men.

But when Ogle looked closely at Dutch, he saw that here was no Tindle. Here was a man who had fought, hurt and in pain, and who would keep on trying to fight. And then there was no more anger in Ogle at Dutch. His satisfaction and an inexplicable pity drowned it out. He said, 'We'll go now.'

Dutch spat at him. 'Go to hell.'

'Perhaps I will,' Ogle agreed. 'I'm sorry I shot your horse,' he added.

Dutch stayed where he was. Ogle watched him for a moment and then went for his horse and came back. He said, 'It will be easier if you help. If not, it will hurt.' He took a rope and dropped a loop about Dutch.

It was obvious that Dutch did not understand Ogle's attempt at kindness and so he fought it. When Ogle was done, Dutch was lashed so that his arms were tied tightly but his legs were free. Ogle tied the loose end of the rope to the cantle of his saddle and mounted. He rode slowly so that Dutch could keep up. Now and then the man tried to hold back but the pressure of the rope squeezing against his broken arm forced him to keep moving.

At Carr's house, Ogle dismounted and led Dutch toward the door. It came open and Milo appeared, a gun in his hand.

Ogle called out his own name, and Milo

came forward slowly, warily. Ogle explained what had happened and what he had done. Milo listened in silence, his expression showing that he was not convinced of this. Having Dutch tied as he was made it easier for Ogle to prove what he was saying.

Finally he cried, 'Don't believe me. But I tell you that Carr and Pat Tyler are boxed up there by the sheriff and Griff.'

'So?'

'I'm going to get Purvis and Dyke and try to help them.'

Milo indicated Dutch. 'What about him?'

'He's a witness,' Ogle said. 'When he tells the truth of it, then the sheriff will believe us.'

Dutch laughed, a harsh, jeering sound. Milo swung on him, a hand raised. Then he turned again to Ogle. 'All right. One of the boys will watch this joker. I'm riding with you.'

'Hurry,' was all Ogle said. He started for the barn.

He left his horse to rest, taking one from Carr's coral, and when Milo and Rick had joined him, rode for Purvis' house.

When Purvis came awake enough to understand what was happening, he hurried to dress. Ogle left the T-Over men to saddle a horse for Purvis and rode to get Jerry Dyke. All five met on the trail that joined Ogle's and Dyke's places and then hurried as fast as the night and the terrain would permit toward the trail that followed the west ridge.

'What if Griff and his crew fight?' Dyke asked Ogle.

'We fight,' Ogle said quietly. 'What else is there for us do? I've attacked two of Griff's men—and Dutch is a deputy, I suppose. I'm an outlaw to the sheriff.' After a moment, he added, 'But we fight only if they have Carr and Pat Tyler.'

There was no answer as each man accepted this, and they went on in silence with Ogle in the lead. It was in his mind to get back to the head of Rustler's Trail and perhaps squeeze the sheriff and his men from the rear. It never occurred to Ogle that Carr might not have tried to hold out against the law.

At the fork marked by the clump of firs, Ogle stopped to draw them all into a bunch. From beside him, Purvis said, 'Listen . . .'

In the near distance there were the sounds of horses coming. They made a rhythm, slow and steady, as if a good-sized group was picking its way warily through the waning moonlight.

'Into the timber,' Ogle ordered.

They drew back, some in the firs, some in the pines across the trail. Shortly the riders appeared, black blobs in the last of the moonlight.

Ogle said softly to Milo beside him, 'Eight of them—and four roped in their saddles.' As the riders came level with him, he made out that three of those roped to their horses rode with their heads up. The fourth man slumped, wobbling from side to side as if he might be badly wounded.

'That's Nash and Griff in the lead,' Milo whispered.

'Follow me!' Ogle kicked at his horse and burst from the timber, his gun out. 'Rein in! Rein in, all of you.'

The men riding free swung about, startled at the suddenness of this. Griff went for his gun and then stopped as he became aware of men flanking him on either side. Slowly his hands went up. The others followed suit.

'What is the meaning of this?' Nash demanded.

'What it looks like,' Ogle said placidly. Inside he was shaking, but his voice was calm. 'Untie that string of horses, Sheriff.'

'The law—'

'The law be damned!' Larry Purvis said shrilly. 'What has the law done but make a fool of itself lately? Untie 'em like he says.'

Silently Nash untied the lead rope from his saddle. It led to Carr, the other horses being tied behind his in the fashion of a pack train.

When his horse was free, Carr directed it with his knees, leading the train around behind Ogle and Milo. He and Rick went to work with their knives, freeing all the men except the one slumped in the saddle. Milo cursed softly, questioningly, when he saw that it was Pat Tyler.

Carr said, 'Leave him tied. He got hit when they raked the timber with their guns. That's why we gave up so fast. He's hurt pretty bad.' He called to the sheriff, 'We'll be obliged if you'll return our guns.' And added dryly, 'Put your own on the ground along with ours.'

There was no movement. Carr reached over and took Ogle's gun from his hand. 'Sheriff,' he said, 'we put up no fight when we were cornered—and you were all targets tonight. We could have shot you a dozen times lately. We knew you were up watching today but we let you go. Remember that.'

He pulled back the hammer of the gun, making a loud sound in the silence. 'You see things your way; we see things ours. Right now, to us, Griff here is a criminal—a land grabber. We'll fight him to get back what he stole from us. And your joining him makes you equally guilty. *Now drop those guns!*'

They came out carefully, carbines and hand guns, thudding softly to the dust of the trail. Then Nash and Griff, with his men, sat unarmed as the gray dawn spread slowly over the sky. The deep chill of early morning crept in, frosting their breaths, numbing them.

'Now ride,' Carr ordered. 'Sometime we'll return your arsenal.'

Nash kept the lead, going toward the switchback and town. Griff hesitated briefly and started to swing off onto the trail that led through Carr's land to the Saddle. With a sudden movement of his horse, Ogle blocked him, and he followed after Nash.

When they were out of sight, Carr got stiffly from the saddle and gathered in the guns. Ogle said, 'Where to?'

'My place,' Carr answered. 'And thanks to all of you.'

'What else could a man do?' Ogle demanded.

'What can we do now?' Purvis asked aloud. 'Nash may be a criminal to us, like Carr says, but before the law we're the criminals. In two more days, Griff will force our beef out of the valley. And there's no way to stop him. No law to stop.'

'One,' Carr said. 'Force. It's all we have left.'

'Griff has over a dozen men,' Milo said. 'Even if we had Nash with us, could we atop Griff now?'

Carr looked at these men and realized more fully than ever that fighting was not a part of them. To brawl on a Saturday night, or even new and then to get stirred up as they had recently, was one thing; to fight a war against trained gunmen was something that none could really conceive.

'We'll have to take the chance of going against Griff—and against the law. It's that or—run.'

He started along the trail to his house. The others fell in line behind him.

Neil Griff, his face drawn with fatigue, set down his coffee cup and looked at Finley. 'We can't hamstring the sheriff forever, Ed. He's got law on the brain but that doesn't mean he's going to be a fool always. If we're going to consolidate our position, we have to do it now.'

Finley nodded ponderously. 'And you've got the ranchers against you. Individually, men like Ogle and Purvis are nothing, but under someone like Lindon they may be a good deal.'

Griff lit a cheroot and stroked his day's growth of whisker. 'I've avoided force as much as possible because I wanted public opinion with me—it would make things easier later. Lindon has been avoiding it because he's never had experience acting outside the law before.' His smile was somber. 'Both of us are going to have to forget that.'

Finley laced his fat fingers together. 'You're going to attack him?'

Griff shook his head. 'I'm going to make him attack me. That's better generalship. I'll make him come out into the open where I can hit him easier.'

'Meaning what?'

Griff said softly, 'The sheriff's sister is in jail for having been on Lindon's side against her brother. If she were to be taken out of jail, the sheriff would be hamstrung. He might even be persuaded to think Lindon got her. And,' he added with more life in his voice, 'Lindon might be persuaded to try and take her away from us.'

Griff rose and went to the stove, where he poured another cup of coffee. Sitting down again, he called out, and a man came in from the other room.

'How's Perly, Shurtleff?'

'The doctor says he'll heal. The shot took him in the fat part of his leg.' Shurtleff swore. 'Dutch ain't come back yet, Boss.'

'Dutch can take care of himself,' Griff answered. 'Right now, I have a job for you and a few of the boys.'

'Going after Lindon and Ogle and them?' Shurtleff looked hopeful.

Griff shook his head. 'Let them stew for a while. When we work this, they'll come after us.' He laughed. 'In fact, I'll say that they'll come running.'

*   *   *

Carr straightened up from the bed where Pat Tyler lay breathing raggedly. 'That's all I can do,' he said. 'It's got worse during the day. We have to get Doc Mason.'

'Any man who goes for the doctor,' Ogle said heavily, 'goes to jail.'

'A chance I have to take,' Carr said. 'It'll be after dark, though.' He went into the parlor, followed by Ogle. Milo and Peak were out guarding. The rest were asleep wherever they could find room. Carr went on to the kitchen.

When he had come in that morning, he had found Dutch roped in a chair, guarded by Bill Marcus. Now, with the day nearly gone, Dutch was still there, slumped wearily in the ropes that held him, but as silent as ever.

'When you get ready to speak your piece to the sheriff,' Carr told him, 'we'll ease up on you.'

Dutch managed a taunting grin but did not answer. Carr moved about the kitchen, preparing a meal. When the food was ready, he waked the men and fed them. Afterwards, they moved to the parlor, away from Dutch.

Carr said, 'Any of your hands that might want to go in with us?' He looked at Ogle.

'This isn't their quarrel,' Ogle answered. 'I can count on only one.'

'Purvis?'

Purvis shrugged. 'Between us, Jerry and me use only two hands. You know that. I wouldn't count on either man in a fight.'

'Ten men, then,' Carr said, 'not counting Pat. If it comes to a showdown, that may mean something.' His smile was grim. 'Maybe I should say, '*When* it comes to a showdown.'

Ogle went off to see if he could get one man from his place to join them. Ned Watts and Rick Bettle relieved Milo and Peak at guard, and the others lay down to sleep until dark.

183

There had been no disturbance, either from Griff or the sheriff, and Carr was puzzled by this. He was also grateful for the respite.

At dark, Ned Watts awakened the men and Carr prepared to go to town. 'Watch for Doc Mason,' he warned. 'Don't go shooting a man just because he rides this way.'

'Going alone don't make sense,' Peak said. 'If I was—'

Ned Watts opened his mouth. 'Shut up,' he said.

Carr rode to town by way of the switchback, leaving his horse in a clump of trees not far from the doctor's house and going the rest of the way on foot. He slipped in at the back, not knocking but entering through the dark kitchen. He stood near the closed parlor door, listening to make certain there were no visitors.

He heard nothing and called out. In a moment the door opened and Doctor Mason came in. He held a lighted lamp in one hand, a gun in the other. He was fully dressed even to his hat.

'Ah, it's you,' he said, seeing Carr. He lowered the gun. 'I was up to Griff's today and I heard Tyler'd been shot. Nash will keep an eye on this place, expecting you.'

'It looks as if you were expecting someone too, Doc. Why the gun?'

'Two reasons. I was going after Bette. She pried it out of me a little while ago that Pat is

184

hurt and she rode off to find him.'

'While he was conscious.' Carr murmured, 'Pat was wondering how she felt about him now.'

'A woman can look below the surface of things,' the doctor said. 'She feels no differently than she did.'

'And the other reason for the gun?' Carr reminded him.

'For Griff's men. What I saw up there, I didn't like. Nash is being a fool in this, and I told him so. A range war isn't my affair—except that I'll have to do the patching up. But this town is my concern, and Nash is letting the power slip into the hands of a man like Griff.'

'You've been talking to someone,' Carr said. He took the time to make a cigarette.

'I've been talking to Elsa Nash,' Mason answered. He held the lamp out for Carr to use in lighting his cigarette. 'Where is Pat?'

'My place. I came for you.'

The doctor nodded. 'Bette will go there first, I think.'

'And you didn't try to stop her?'

The doctor snorted disgustedly. 'Ever try to do anything with a woman in love?' His shrewd eyes measured Carr. 'Speaking of women in love, Elsa is in the jailhouse.'

'So Ogle told me.' Carr started for the door. 'I'm going there now, Doc. We have one of Griff's men at my place. He has a broken arm. A man in that shape can't keep silent forever.

Maybe the sheriff would like to be there when he talks.'

'You'll have to take him at gunpoint, Carr.'

'If so, then he wouldn't believe what he heard,' Carr said. 'I'll try, anyway.'

He slipped out the way he had come. Getting his own horse, he rode through the darkness to the Nash barn. On his way he saw Doctor Mason leaving. Slipping from his horse at the barn, he walked toward the one lighted cell, coming in from the side so that the glow wouldn't reveal him to anyone watching. When he was beneath the window, he called, 'Elsa?'

She came to the window. 'Carr? Carr, you idiot.'

He moved closer and reached up so that their hands met. 'Can you stand being in a while longer?'

'As long as you're all right . . .'

'I could take you with me,' he said.

'A woman is only a hindrance to a man running or fighting,' she answered.

His hand squeezed down on hers, thanking her for her understanding. Then he said, 'I came to see your brother, Elsa.'

'Carr, Sim is half crazy after what you did last night. He's ready to shoot you on sight, Doctor Mason told me.'

'No one will shoot,' he said. 'Get him for me, Elsa.'

She turned away and he heard her calling,

186

'Sim, Sim.'

Carr slipped to the outside door. It was locked as he had expected. He heard footsteps, then Nash's voice: 'Well?'

'Carr is here,' she said. 'Under the window. He wants to talk to you.'

Nash must have emotions, after all, Carr thought. He heard the cell door clang back, heard heavy, hurried steps race for the window. Then there was silence. Carr understood its meaning when Elsa said, 'This is your gun I'm holding, Sim. You get careless when you hurry. Now go let Carr in. He wants to talk, not have a gun fight.'

'I warn you—' Nash began. His voice sounded close to breaking.

'You'll do nothing,' she lashed out at him. 'I have only contempt for you and what you call the law. And I'm capable of shooting what I hold in contempt.'

Carr stepped away from the door and loosened his gun as he heard Nash walk down the hallway. The door came open and Sim Nash was revealed, lamplight at his back.

Carr backed Nash into the cell, against the far wall. Elsa stood near the door, her brother's gun steady in her hand. 'Thank you,' he said to her. 'I could have done it without this.'

'I know. I just wanted him to be sure where I stand.'

Nash stared at them, his expression cold and

unyielding.

Carr said, 'You've refused to listen to anything said to you, Sheriff. And last night you deputized a bunch of range thieves and rustlers. Now you have to listen. You can believe or not as you choose.'

Nash did not answer and Carr went on, detailing what he knew step by step. Nash had heard all this before and his expression did not change. Carr said finally, 'Ogle killed Tindle, by the way—in self-defense. He was bringing Tindle in to have him tell you the story.'

'Dead men make fine witnesses,' Nash said coldly.

'Your privilege to call us liars,' Carr answered quietly: 'But right now, one of Griff's men is at my place. Doc Mason is on his way there. The man has a broken arm and he's hungry. You might find it a chance to question him.'

'To listen to the words you'll make him say—under duress?'

'Are we that kind?' Carr demanded. 'Have we ever been—' He saw that it was hopeless and he stopped. 'Then, no matter what you hear, you can't believe us?'

'No,' Nash said simply.

Carr turned away. 'You can give him his gun back after I get a start—if you wish,' he said to Elsa. He looked back at the sheriff. 'I suggest you think over what I said, Nash.'

'Come to your place and ride into a trap?'

'We could have shot you long before this, Sheriff.' Carr went to Elsa and bent his head to her, kissing her briefly. Their eyes met for only an instant, but in hers Carr saw her love for him and her thanks because he had not taken his advantage to go against her brother. He whispered, 'Don't worry,' and then he was gone.

'Give me my gun, Elsa,' Nash said.

She stood by the door, the gun hanging limply at her side, her eyes contemptuous as she watched him. He paced the cell, then suddenly turned and started for her. 'No farther, Sim!' she warned.

'Give me that gun!'

He came suddenly in a rush of blind rage. She had never seen him lose control like this before and for an instant she stood shocked and startled. Then his hand brushed hers and she moved aside, lifting the gun and slashing down with the barrel.

The blow struck his arm and he twisted aside with pain, his expression incredulous that this could happen. She waited no longer but stepped toward him, changing her grip so that she held the gun by the barrel. She drove the butt with all her strength against the side of his head.

He swiveled toward her, his mouth open in surprise, and then sagged forward, going to his knees, and then falling to his face, where he lay still.

'I'm sorry, Sim,' she said simply. 'You forced it on me.'

She turned and ran to the barn, where she saddled a horse. She left by way of the jail so that she could glance into the cell window as she passed. She could see her brother on his feet, swaying dizzily, groping for the doorway.

Fighting back tears of tension, she urged the horse forward, out of town. She chose to go by way of the Saddle as the barely risen moon cast too little light for her to trust the narrower, dimmer trails when she had no time to waste.

Halfway up the slope, she heard riders coming. She tried to rein off into the timber but they were on her before she could get her horse from the road. A man she had never seen before darted to her side.

'Hey, boys,' he shouted. 'That's service, ain't it? Go after something and it comes to you.' Laughing, he grasped her bridle.

'Let go!' Elsa drew the .38 she wore at her waist. Another man rode in behind her and plucked it from her hand, leaving her helpless.

'Come on, lady,' the first man said. 'There's a fellow up the road wants to see you.'

She tried to free herself again, saw that she was surrounded, and rode silently with them to Griff's.

CHAPTER FOURTEEN

Carr found Doctor Mason in his kitchen. He looked up from setting Dutch's arm. 'You were gone long enough,' he commented. 'The boys were just about ready to go out after you.'

'I was looking over the valley,' Carr said. 'And Griff's. He has a good many guards posted tonight.'

'Expecting someone, maybe,' the doctor said dryly. He stood away from Dutch. 'This one won't talk.'

Carr nodded. He had expected as much. 'How's Pat?' he asked.

'Go see. Bette had him taken care of when I arrived. She's as good a surgeon now as I'll ever be.'

Carr went through the parlor and into the bedroom. Bette Mason was by Tyler's bed, talking to him in low tones. Carr studied her gentle blonde prettiness, thinking how deceptive it was. He told her what her father had said, and she laughed lightly.

'I wanted to learn so I could doctor T-Over cows when the time came.'

'If there is a T-Over,' Tyler said. He looked less drawn, more like himself after the full day's rest and some obviously first-rate treatment.

'I'm going to have Doc take you and Dutch

191

back to town, Pat,' Carr said. 'I think Nash will use Griff to attack us tonight, and we may have to run again.'

'Run—where?'

Carr smiled without much humor. 'Into the valley—to push Griff's beef out.'

Tyler threw back the covers, showing that he was fully clothed except for his boots. Over Bette's protests, he got to his feet and stood on them firmly. 'I can ride and I can handle a gun,' he said. 'It's my fight. It's my ranch Griff has.'

Carr looked at Bette and she nodded almost imperceptibly. 'It's your say, fellow,' he told Pat. 'But it's going to be a rough ride.'

Old Peak was standing in the bedroom doorway. 'I got an idea,' he said. 'Maybe me and Pat could go over to Griff's. I know a spot where we can raise a mite of a fuss. All Pat'll have to do is lie down and shoot.'

'You know Pat better than that,' Carr said. He thought the suggestion over, however, and from it an idea shaped and took form. He called all the men into the parlor.

'Doc, you take Dutch and ride to town. There'll come a time when he might feel like talking to save his own neck.' He nodded to old Peak. 'You and Pat do like you said. If you raise ruckus enough, maybe Griff won't get as well organized as he'd like.'

'And us?' Ogle asked.

'We'll leave the place looking like we're in

192

it,' Carr said. 'But the rest of us'll be in the valley where we have fighting room. By the time Griff finds we aren't here, we can have enough of his beef in the Saddle to give him trouble.'

'Ah,' Ogle said. For the first time in his life, he looked forward to a fight.

They began to ready themselves, first making sure that Doctor Mason got away with Dutch. Carr tried to send Bette as well, but she only shook her head at him.

'This is no place for a woman.'

'I'm Pat's nurse,' she said quietly. 'Where he goes, I go.' Her eyes went to Tyler. 'Or he doesn't go.'

'Get her a gun,' Carr said to Peak.

When they were ready, old Peak and Tyler, with Bette at his side, rode away. The remainder of the crew moved slowly to a spot from which they could make a dash onto the Saddle and into the valley. Carr left his horse and climbed to a watch point and squatted there. He looked through the starkly moonlit night toward the trail sloping gently into the broad, still valley.

Down below, at the top of the Saddle, two men patrolled. They rode back and forth, alert, guns across their laps. Carr studied them for a while and then slipped back and outlined their next move. He sent Ned Watts up to watch, and the men settled down to wait for the signal to ride.

Elsa Nash sat on the bed in the small room where she had been put and studied the man guarding her. He sat by the door, his gun carelessly in his lap. He had a thick bandage puffing through the slit that had been made in a leg of his jeans, and he sat with that leg thrust straight out in front of him. His big blondness made her realize that this was the man who had impersonated Pat Tyler.

She spoke to him, drawing him out, getting him to boast of the trick he had worked. When she had all the information to corroborate Ogle's story, she wondered what she would do with it. No information that she had was of any value unless Sim could be made to believe it.

The sudden sound of his voice coming from the next room startled her. For a moment she thought she was imagining it, that the concentration of her thought on him had tricked her, but when he spoke again, she realized that he was there. She looked at the guard, remembering he had been called Perly, and noticed that he was listening too.

Nash's voice was clear and sharp. 'I came for help again. Lindon and his men are at his place. As a deputized officer of the law, it's your duty to help me arrest them.'

'We tried that once, Sheriff,' Griff rumbled. 'Let them stew a while. They'll hang

194

themselves.'

'As the law, I demand—'

Griff laughed at him. 'Sheriff, you may as well know it. To me, your law is a joke. I'll get rid of Lindon when I'm ready. I have no intention of attacking him—I'm going to make him attack me.'

Elsa listened to no more. Seeing that Perly was absorbed in the talk from the other room, she made a desperate leap for the table where the lamp stood. By the time he managed to turn around, she had the light blown out. She dropped to the floor in the darkness.

'Sim! Sim!' She rolled as she called. There was a gunshot and she heard the bullet gouge the floor where she had lain. The gun went off again, and the lamp chimney shattered.

The door was flung open and light streamed in. Elsa saw her brother standing there, bewilderment on his features. He noticed her at the same time that she cried out in warning. Perly had his gun lifted again, drawing his bead on her.

Nash turned. His arm slashed out, knocking Perly sideways, making his shot go into the ceiling. He started toward Elsa, and then stopped as Griff stepped up behind him and pressed a gun hard against his back.

'Raise your hands, Sheriff.' He lifted Nash's gun from its holster and pushed him on into the room. Then he swung viciously on Perly.

'Get out, you butchering fool. Who told you

to shoot at a woman? Send Shurtleff in here.'

Perly limped out and in a moment Shurtleff lumbered in. Griff ordered him to stand guard. Nash was helping Elsa to her feet. When she was seated on the bed again, he stepped toward Griff. 'What's the meaning of this? Of having her here?'

'Why,' Griff said in a smooth voice, 'she just came. Sheriff.'

'They caught me on the trail,' Elsa said, interrupting. 'They were riding to town to get me out of jail—and make you think Carr had done it.' She could see the color climb up her brother's neck. 'They plan to use me for bait—to bring Carr into the open. To trap him.'

Griff shrugged. 'It makes no difference now, Sheriff. I've already told you what I think of your law.' He turned and went out, shutting the door behind him.

His voice could be heard rumbling at Finley: 'It's moving too fast to wait now, Ed. Let's get a message to Lindon that we have his woman. We're more ready for an attack than he is to make one.'

Sim Nash sat heavily beside his sister, his face in his hands. She reached out, putting her arms around him. 'Now you know,' she said almost gently.

'Now I know,' he said. He made it sound as if he were cursing himself.

From the other room came Griff's voice giving orders: 'Get that message started, Ed.

The rest of you come with me. We'll line the timber along the road in here. Let them get almost to the house and then—hit them. Perly, you stay and get them from the front.'

Elsa sat silently, looking at Shurtleff and seeing nothing there that might help. She heard the sounds the men made as they departed. Then they were gone. About a dozen, she thought, and every man a trained gun fighter, every man bought by Griff for one purpose—to kill when there was killing to be done.

Shurtleff jerked his gun. 'Separate, you two. And keep your hands in sight. I don't object to shooting a woman no more'n Perly.'

The minutes dragged. The sounds of men riding off had faded, leaving only heavy silence. Then a gun went off shatteringly near by. It's come, she thought. Shurtleff did not move, but kept his eyes fixed on her and her brother.

Another gun barked. Then another. A fusillade came and the sounds of the bullets ripping into the house could be heard. Now Shurtleff started up.

'What the hell are they doing on this side of the house?'

Lead smashed through the windowpane, scattering glass into the room and making Shurtleff dive for cover. He lifted his head just in time to see Nash coming across the room at him. The gun in his hand slammed viciously.

Nash jerked but kept on coming, his body driving Shurtleff to the wall, pinning him there. Elsa was on her feet, running. Shurtleff was caught in Nash's grip now and he was bucking like a crazed steer. She reached out and caught his gun and held on. It was like clutching a snapping whip. Nash let loose his grip suddenly and Shurtleff fell forward, across Elsa. Nash slashed down against Shurtleff's neck with his fist. Elsa stumbled as the gun came out of Shurtleff's lax fingers and he pitched to the floor.

Outside the firing had ceased but the beat of hoofs was close. She ran to the broken window, calling out in warning, 'Carr!'

The hoofbeats stopped. 'Who's there?' It was as old man's voice.

'It's Peak,' Nash said. He was tying Shurtleff with the man's own belt. Done, he stood up and joined Elsa at the window. She put out an arm, thrusting him back.

'They'll shoot you as fast as they will Griff now,' she warned. She called again, 'It's Elsa Nash. Where is Carr?'

Peak rode up close to the window. 'All right,' he said. 'We saw Griff ride out. Where'd he—'

She broke in, talking rapidly, warning him about the trap. Peak laughed, a high-pitched cackle, and lifted his arm in a signal. Through the dim light coming by way of the parlor window next to where she stood, Elsa saw Pat

Tyler and a smaller figure approaching.

Peak said, 'Griff and his crew only went to the road. They're waiting for Carr to hit this place.'

'Let's ride then,' Tyler said. 'Our work is done here.' He gave his attention to Elsa. 'What about you?'

From beside her, but out of the line of vision, Nash said, 'We can make it.'

The men stiffened at his voice. Elsa cried, 'Wait! Sim understands now. Tell Carr that.'

Tyler started to speak and stopped as the sound of horses coming rose on the night air. Peak said, 'Griff. We don't have that many men. Our shots musta drew him.'

The small figure near Tyler moved closer and Elsa recognized Bette Mason. 'Come through the window,' Bette urged them both. 'There's no time for anything else.'

'There's another man—' Elsa began.

Old Peak was out of the saddle and at the window. Elsa pushed it up and started through. Peak was cackling again. 'That other man must be the one Bette picked off the veranda. Shoots like a veteran.'

Elsa jumped easily to the ground with his help and turned to her brother. He half slid, half fell over the sill to the ground. She gave a small cry and bent to give him a hand but he struggled to his feet without assistance. 'Just scraped my side,' he said harshly. 'Shurtleff is a poor shot.'

They rode double, Elsa and Nash taking Bette's horse and Bette climbing up with old Peak. The beat of the oncoming horses was louder now, dangerously close. Tyler led the way, swinging into timber on top of a knoll that looked down on the house. From there they could see Griff and his crew streaming into the yard, sweeping about the house.

'Hope Carr got down there,' Peak said. 'Griff ain't going to sit and gawk long at an empty house. In a minute he'll turn and hit for the valley. Carr'd better be ready.'

Carr had his men strung out. They were driving southward a large herd that had been pastured near the foot of the Saddle. Old Peak's shooting at T-Over had pulled the guards in that direction, and Carr had run his crew into the valley. Now he could hear nothing but the lowing of cattle, the movements of horses.

Then he heard them coming. They rode fast and hard, the stomping of their horses shaking the ground. Carr cried, 'Run that beef into the Saddle—on the double!'

Men moved swiftly in the moonlight. The bunched cattle were pointed for the Saddle, forced into awkward, shambling runs that carried them up the first slope. Guns went off behind them, sharp, harsh sounds that sent them surging in panic.

Carr pressed along with the rest, his attention beyond, on the crest. He saw riders appear there, silhouetted in the moonlight. The man in the lead dipped downward, and then the rest followed.

'Watch it! Don't let them turn the herd and trap you. Watch it!'

Griff and his men came down two abreast, riding like a small army. Halfway down the slope they met the first of the cattle and now it was Griff's voice that rose on the air:

'Turn them!'

A gun blasted. The flowing wave of cattle, confronted with this wall of men and horses, hesitated. A second gunshot decided them. Slowly, despite the pressure from behind, the leaders swung about and began to run, lowing wildly, back to the valley.

Carr spread his men out quickly, pulling them up the sloping sides of the lower part of the Saddle. 'Five minutes more and they would have been a weapon,' he said bitterly. Now the cattle were nothing. It had been a gamble that had been lost, and Carr knew he had lost any chance to maneuver his men for an attack on Griff's larger forces.

Griff and his crew were too numerous, too powerful, for his slender force to try to hold down in the valley. He had to break them now or not at all.

He moved toward Milo and called his order above the thunder of the running cattle. The word was passed along, and then the men settled back in the deepness of the shadows and waited.

Griff's crew, strung out now, rode after the tail of the herd, still firing, half-screened by the thick cloud of dust.

Carr's voice lifted suddenly above the noise. 'Now!'

His gun blasted as the crew came level with him. A man cried out somewhere in pain and surprise. Another gun flashed. Griff's voice rose again: 'Turn and hit them! Break them!'

Those coming down the Saddle scattered, ghostlike figures in the mingled dust and moonlight. They shot as they moved, and beside Carr a man jerked in the saddle and pitched to the ground. He kept firing at the elusive riders, moving to keep his gun flashes from being a target, not sure he was hitting anything.

Griff and most of his crew hit the bottom of the slope, turned, and started up again. When Carr saw that most of them had gone down, he had felt a surge of hopelessness, knowing that his puny attack had failed. But now he saw that Griff's driving anger, his tremendous self-assurance, had turned the man about, was bringing him back as Carr wanted it.

Griff had his men in a line, combing the dark pockets of the side slopes as they came. Carr reined his horse in tightly and steadied his gun. His own men, he knew, were waiting, each doing as he was, each knowing that one shot would bring three in return, and knowing,

202

too, that there was no other answer than to make that one shot.

They started down, guns flaming as they came. Carr heard a grunted curse next to him. It was Mort Ogle. 'How many men has he got?' he demanded wonderingly.

The answer came in a shrill yell, a high-pitched cackle. 'That's not Griff's men,' Carr answered. 'It's Peak. Squeeze them!' he shouted. 'Now!'

He led his crew out, forming a crescent around the end of Griff's line. From the other side of the slope, Jerry Dyke appeared, following the same pattern. Peak and his few pressed down from the top—and Griff's crew broke.

'Go through them!' Griff cried. Then his voice was lost in the surge of sound, of guns slamming, horses neighing, of men crying in pain or triumph. The dust swirled up, dancing in the moonlight.

Momentarily it cleared where Carr rode and he saw Peak ahead. Pat Tyler materialized beside him, one hand clinging to the horn of his saddle. A gun cracked and Tyler's horse pitched forward, sending the rider into the air and then out of sight in the dust.

Carr reined about, saw a .44 muzzle coming down, and fired. The man grunted and seemed to slide backward as his horse darted forward with an empty saddle. Carr turned again and was brought up sharply against another rider.

203

He lifted his gun to fire.

'Carr!' It was Elsa Nash, her .38 in her hand, her hair blown and wild from the force of her ride.

His gun lowered. 'Get out of here,' he said almost harshly. 'You—' He broke off as another figure loomed up. 'Ride, Elsa.' His gun lifted again.

She flung herself forward, blocking him. 'That's Sim! Carr, he knows—now.'

Carr saw Nash shoot above him, behind him, and he turned to get a glimpse of one of Griff's men veering off, then trying to straighten out, and finally dropping from the saddle to lie spread-eagled in the dirt.

The dust thinned and Carr could make out the remnants of Griff's crew as they formed a spearhead and drove downslope toward him. He tried to ride to where Elsa and her brother were, to force her away from the fight, but they had drifted away and now four men were cutting a line between them and Carr. Griff bulked large in the lead, his gun spreading a screen of lead as he rode.

Nash stood his ground, a rifle in his hands answering Griff's challenge. Off to the sides, scattered, Carr could hear the backwash of the battle. But the core was here—in Neil Griff— and so he joined Nash, driving through the hail of Griff's lead. He shouted at Elsa, who rode slightly behind them, ordering her away. But she only lined up her gun and fired coolly.

One of the four went out of the saddle. Carr heard a bullet tick the rim of his hat and he fired at the rider. The man shot twice more as he was falling, and then he disappeared into the dust.

Griff's horse came on. Carr heard the impact as it struck Nash's mount, and the two men went down together. Elsa cried a warning to Carr, and her small gun made its sharp sound, and the last of the four pitched free as his horse stumbled and fell, neighing in pain.

Carr had a glimpse of Griff rising from the dust. He reached out and caught a riderless horse milling nearby and swung down for the vast darkness of the valley.

'See to your brother,' Carr called to Elsa, and then he was gone, driving after Griff.

He followed Griff's progress as the man twisted through a still-milling herd of cattle. Then Griff swung to his left, toward the darkness that lay against the west side of the valley. Carr reined his tired horse, making a wide arc around the beef that had slowed Griff. The moonlight was entirely gone where they rode, cut off by the west ridge.

Carr saw the dark blob that was Griff stop and turn. Then his gun flamed brightly in the deep, pre-dawn blackness. The shot was wide, singing away to Carr's left. He answered it, and Griff fired again. This time Carr heard the close whine of the bullet and he edged his horse off at an angle, shooting as he moved.

205

Griff's horse pitched as Carr's bullet nicked it. Griff went up and backward. Carr kicked spurs to his spraddle-legged mount and sent it forward. Griff was getting up from the ground, his hands empty. He raised them high.

'All right,' Carr said. He left his horse and walked to where Griff stood. Seeing that Griff's holster was empty, he unbuckled his own gun belt and tossed it to one side.

Griff laughed. He was still laughing when Carr stepped forward and drove the sound back into his teeth. Griff stopped laughing and ducked as Carr swung another fist. He brought his own left into Carr's ribs and drove a right to the side of Carr's head.

Carr went down, stayed briefly on one knee, and then rose again. Griff hit him as he came in. He did not stop but let Griff punish him until he was in close. Then he took both fists and slammed them into Griff's middle. Griff gasped and backed off. Carr moved in, slugging, not seeming to feel the blows Griff rained on him.

Griff kept backing now, sucking for air as Carr's fists ripped out his wind. One blow took his throat and he gagged and stopped. A looping right smashed against his jaw. Carr could feel the man's bone break under the impact as he went down.

Carr waited, his hands hanging limply, the blood running from his nose and lips. Griff got slowly to his feet and moved sideways, and

Carr went after him. Griff stood with his guard down. When Carr hit him again, he fell and rolled. He came up with his own gun in his hand.

'That's enough, Lindon.' His voice was thick, the words said with an effort. He fired.

Carr felt the bullet, cold ice and fire, streak across his side. He was leaping with the shot, and his foot lashed out, kicking the gun from Griff's hand. He reached down, grabbed a fistful of shirt, and pulled.

Griff came to his feet, striking out weakly, and Carr rammed his blow forward with all the strength he had left, putting his weight and fury and hatred at this latest treachery into his fist. Griff's face dissolved in a smear of spurting blood and he dropped like an animal pole-axed.

Carr turned and stumbled about until he found his own gun. He belted it on and turned, waiting. Griff stirred, got slowly to his knees, and stayed there, looking at Carr.

'You're beat,' Carr said. 'You're beat both ways, Griff. Your men are gone, shot or run off. Even your friend Finley is gone. I saw him squirming in the dirt back there. You haven't got anything left, Griff. Get your gun.'

Griff turned, still on his knees, and crawled to where his gun lay. He put a hand on it and started to push himself upright. Before he was fully erect, he swiveled about, shooting as he moved.

Carr kept his hand loose at his side. The bullet plowed into the grass at his feet and died there. He said, 'You had me if you'd chosen to risk a fair chance, Griff. Even beat as you are, you're a faster man with a gun.' He continued to wait, letting Griff stand straight, letting him raise his gun for another shot. Then he drew, firing as his own gun cleared leather.

Griff took a step forward, looked down at himself, at the spreading stain on his chest, and fell. He lay face down, his hands outthrust, reaching toward the new dawn coming over the east cliffs.

Carr walked to him, his gun hanging limply in his fingers. He stopped and looked down at the body. 'You're beat,' he said. He fell face down across Griff and did not move.

*   *   *

Pat Tyler lay in the bed next to him in Doc Mason's crowded 'hospital.' As Carr told him, he would be glad when Tyler went home as he was sick of his and Bette's mooning. Tyler pointed out that he felt the same way, since Elsa Nash spent more time here than she did at home.

Doc Mason told them both to shut up. He added that he didn't see how either of them had managed to live, but since they had, they would both have to go home soon to make room for more deserving cases.

Every time he examined Carr, he shook his head in wonder. 'They lost seven and the rest disappeared, I hear. You got five men hurt, but you're the worst of the lot. Why'd you have to pick a fight with that bruiser?'

'My way of doing it,' Carr said through bruised lips. 'Has my visitor come yet?'

Doc Mason snorted, sounding like old Peak. 'What you want to entertain a woman for, with your mouth all beat up like that?' He stumped out, leaving Pat Tyler laughing softly from the next bed.

Elsa came shortly and Sim Nash was with her. Nash stopped by the bed and looked down. 'Ogle and the others asked me to stay on as sheriff,' he said. 'I've resigned. What is your opinion?'

'The same as theirs,' Tyler said.

Carr looked at Elsa and reached for her hand. 'I'd be set up to have the sheriff as my brother-in-law,' he said.

Elsa bent and kissed him, and Carr scarcely noticed how badly bruised his lips were. Nash cleared his throat. 'I'd better get back to my lawing then.' For the first time, Carr saw him smile. Then he couldn't see anything. Elsa's hair was over his eyes.

She straightened up. 'You might propose to me, not to my brother.'

Tyler laughed again. Carr said comfortably, 'Nash is the law. Around here the law has all the say.'

From the doorway, Nash's voice came dryly, 'The law says "yes."'

The door closed softly. Pat Tyler took one look at the next bed and looked politely away. It made no difference. Neither Elsa nor Carr was aware of him.

We hope you have enjoyed this Large Print book. Other Chivers Press or Thorndike Press Large Print books are available at your library or directly from the publishers.

For more information about current and forthcoming titles, please call or write, without obligation, to:

Chivers Large Print
published by BBC Audiobooks Ltd
St James House, The Square
Lower Bristol Road
Bath BA2 3SB
UK
email: bbcaudiobooks@bbc.co.uk
www.bbcaudiobooks.co.uk

OR

Thorndike Press
295 Kennedy Memorial Drive
Waterville
Maine 04901
USA
www.gale.com/thorndike
www.gale.com/wheeler

All our Large Print titles are designed for easy reading, and all our books are made to last.

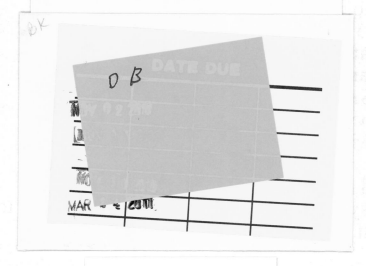